MW01094705

The Piper Sniper:

A Travel Writer Cozy Mystery

By Kelly Young

Kelly Young

Text copyright © 2018 Kelly K Young

All rights reserved

All rights reserved

Young & Keele Press

Author's Note

Please be aware that this book uses Canadian spelling. Not because I am incapable of using American spelling, but because I am too attached to my extra u's and my zeds. You can pry my superfluous u's from my cold, dead keyboard.

You are intelligent people. I'm sure you can handle it.

The photograph on the front cover is of the iconic Kincardine lighthouse. The photo was taken, by yours truly, from the boardwalk on Station Beach and you can see some boats in the harbour through the tall vegetation in the foreground. It is this structure which features prominently in the novel. Each summer evening a bagpiper serenades the setting of the sun with the plaintive strains of his or her instrument from atop the lighthouse.

While it wasn't initially my intention, it is serendipitous that this book will be released the year of the 2018 Kincardine Old Boys & Girls Reunion. The event is held every 10 years. I was fortunate enough to have been in town for two of them, once as a reporter and the second time as a resident participating in the frivolity.

Also, while the town of Kincardine, locations within it, and certain characters are very real, I have taken liberties and artistic licence with some aspects of life in the small town to make the story flow better. My apologies go out to any Kincardine folks who might take offence, as none is intended.

Dedication

As always, this is for my husband Jeff, who keeps coming up with neat ideas that sprout to life between my pen and paper. Also, thank you for helping me develop the character of my cantankerous detective. I love you!

Acknowledgements

This book could not have happened without the help and patience of a number of people.

- My husband Jeff, who gave me a great idea years ago, which sat in the recesses of my mind until I discovered the Cozy Mystery genre.
- Lynn Brown, my proof-reader extraordinaire. Merci Beaucoup, Mon Amie!
- Bonney Green, for volunteering to be a Beta reader.
- Kendrick Shepherd and Charlie Schumacker, for their willingness to share their firearms knowledge with me.
- Matt 'Mattl' (pronounced like 'tattle') Leyden, who was kind enough to tell me of his experience as a 'Phantom Piper', and is rewarded by serving as the first victim of the book.
- All of the wonderful Cozy Mystery writers in whose books I immersed myself for inspiration.
- The Municipality of Kincardine, both for providing the setting and for employing me while I wrote this and a few of my other books.
- The residents of Kincardine who may or may not show up in these pages.

Playlist

In recognition of the Municipality of Kincardine's Scottish Heritage, I have made a list of music that will get you in the spirit for a mystery set in the Scottish town on the shores of Lake Huron.

- The Glengarry Bhoys - http://www.glengarrybhoys.com/ - according to their website, are "Celtic Stompers" with "a hybrid of Canadian Highland Scots and French Canadian music idioms". This Celtic Fusion band is from Glengarry County in Ontario. I heard them at the Kincardine Scottish Festival years ago, and I can tell you they are a lot of fun to see in person.
- The Mudmen - http://www.mudmen.ca/ - billed as Canada's Celtic Rock Warriors; this five-man band from Ontario has also made appearances at Kincardine's Scottish Festival. They are a big draw and their music can be heard on Xbox and PlayStation games.
- The Trews - http://www.thetrewsmusic.com/ - an Eastern Canadian hard and alternative rock band from Antigonish, Nova Scotia. They have wowed the crowds at the Kincardine Scottish Festival, been nominated for Juno awards. They have won East Coast Music Awards in Canada, and Independent Music Awards in the US.
- Dan Stacey and The Black Swans - http://www.danstaceyandtheblackswans.ca - a three man band out of Stratford Ontario. They combine original compositions with Ottawa Valley step dancing and Celtic, Irish, and French classics to put on a unique and highly

entertaining show. This is an up and coming band you will want to keep an eye on!

- Great Big Sea - https://www.youtube.com/user/GreatBigSeaOfficial - a Canadian folkrock band from Newfoundland and Labrador. Their original tunes and versions of traditional folk songs drawing from Irish, Scottish, and Cornish heritage are excellent. I have seen them in concert a number of times and, in true Newfoundland style, they always get folks on their feet.

The Travelling Klutz

"Write what you know." That's what teachers and professors have told students of writing since people began to put chisel to rock.

I (finally, some would say) took that advice to heart as I undertook what I hoped to be my final career change in a long history of career changes.

My name is Casey Robertson and I am the writer of a brand new column 'The Travelling Klutz'. A retired reporter, I sold the idea of the column to Our Ontario, a glossy monthly magazine showcasing the glories of places and things in our province. With a retainer in hand, I was left to ponder where in the province to travel and highlight first.

And so I found myself considering what I know. Jim, my handsome hubby of 34 years, might chuckle at that, but I do know things. And I know places. So, it came to pass that I turned to the small town of Kincardine on the shores of Lake Huron. It had been home for three decades before we retired to a milder climate in south western Ontario.

I was fairly certain writing my first travel article about Kincardine would go well, as I had worked as a reporter covering the local news in various local papers for 20 years.

In a nutshell, I have the skills and I love to travel around the province. It seemed to be a perfect fit for me to take on travel writing.

Kincardine was built around the spot where the Penetagore River flowed into Lake Huron, one of the Great Lakes. I say flowed because not long after settling, one prominent hotel owner had the river diverted so that it would pass nearer his property. The town has plenty of interesting historic facts like that. It has become a major summer tourist spot thanks to its incredible view of sunsets over the lake; vast beaches; a marina within walking distance of the downtown; superb water sports including sailing, paddle boarding, and even surfing; a thriving artistic culture including both professional and amateur theatre; a vast number of recreational choices; and a population known for its welcoming nature.

Going to our old stomping grounds seemed to be a no-brainer.

Thus it was that my first column saw my klutzy self, with handsome hubby in tow, travelling to Kincardine, Ontario. Because, I reasoned, the town is the epitome of what I know. Of course, when you go to a place you know, be prepared to bump into people you know and who know you.

And I mean that quite literally.

Chapter 1

As we strolled down Harbour Street toward the iconic Kincardine Lighthouse, I inadvertently bumped shoulders with a person going the opposite direction. And by 'bumped shoulders', I mean I crashed into and almost knocked that person down. The only thing keeping me on my feet was the steadying hand of my husband.

"OMG! Casey? What are you doing back here?"

I turned to face the woman I had just crashed into. Almost as tall as my 5'10", my old friend, colleague, and editor Marie Battler fixed her brown eyes on me in surprise. Her short black hair, now streaked with a bit more gray than it had been when we last met, ruffled in the fresh breeze off the lake, but you could still see some beads of perspiration on her brow. She had clearly been rushing around in the 28 degree Celsius heat, likely following a story for the paper, her cargo shorts and tank top doing little to keep her cool. Despite the heat, she carried a takeout coffee in one hand, likely not the first one of her day, and a huge bag hung from her shoulder.

"Did you just OMG me?" I asked, tossing back my brown curls that perennially fell into my face, only to have them fall instantly into my eyes again. I was surprised to hear her using the current term. After all, she was a few years my senior and I didn't use that term myself.

"Hey!" Marie answered as she pulled me into a quick hug. "I'm up on the jargon." She looked over my shoulder at the tall, gracefully graying man standing behind me with a bemused look on his face. "Hi Jim," she greeted my husband with a wave. "I see you still have that older Kevin Costner look going for you."

She turned back to give me the once over. "And you're still rocking the leggings, I see," she commented on my usual relaxed look of leggings, pulled up into capris, matched with a flowing tank top.

"They're comfortable," I told her. "You should try a pair."

She shook her head. "No pockets."

"What do you need pockets for?" I teased, pointing to her bag. "You have your suitcase."

"It's a camera bag."

"Sure it is. You keep telling yourself that."

She ignored my jibe and changed the subject. "I never thought I'd see the two of you back in town."

"You and me both," Jim groused in reply, earning a quick, playful slap on the shoulder from me. "But Casey is on assignment." He accented the last word with air quotes, but this time he was quick enough to jump out of the way of the slap headed in his direction.

"Really?" Marie's curiosity was evident in her tone. She motioned to a nearby bench. "Do tell!"

I didn't have to be asked twice, as excited as I was with this new endeavour. I moved to sit on the wooden slat bench at the intersection of Harbour Street and Huron Terrace, draping my camera bag over the cast iron end that formed an elaborate arm rest. I took a moment to take in the view of the white and red lighthouse across the street, and then looked at the old restored Walker House hotel kitty-corner to where we sat. It was a very peaceful, familiar view, and I smiled remembering all the stories I had covered for Marie about the two tourist attractions over the years.

"I'm doing a travel series for *Our Ontario* magazine," I told her.

"And you thought Kincardine was the best place to start?" she asked with a hint of disbelief in her voice as she dropped her large 'camera bag' on the bench and sat down beside me. The bag landed with a clunk, reminding me that it was much more than a conveyance for mere photographic equipment. I had often teased her that it was the Dr. Who 'Tardis' of reporters' bags.

I shrugged. "Write what you know, right? I'm sure someone used to tell me that."

Marie smiled at the memory that comment evoked. "I can't imagine who," she deadpanned. "What is the column going to be called?"

Jim snorted behind me, causing Marie to raise her eyebrows with curiosity. I shot him an annoyed look and he suddenly became engrossed in watching a member of the Kincardine Scottish Pipe Band walk past. Handsome in full regalia, including the blue Kincardine tartan kilt, the young man was clearly on his way to the lighthouse. To be fair, Jim was not the only person watching the piper. He was turning more than a few heads as ladies admired his trim, muscular form, his boy-next-door good looks, and the smile he favoured them with as he caught their eyes. He was likely the band member whose turn it was to climb the spiral staircase to the top of the lighthouse and out onto the small balcony. There he would pipe down the sun in this annual summer tradition unique to the town. It was the reason we were here: to take some photos for my new column.

"Come on," Marie cajoled. "Tell me the name of the column." She was trying, and failing, to catch Jim's eye. He continued to ignore us in favour of watching the nearby crowd.

The deserter. He would definitely hear about that later.

I took a deep breath and prepared myself for her expected reaction. Still, I couldn't resist waiting for her to take a drink of her coffee before I gave in. "Fine," I said. "It's called 'The Travelling Klutz'."

Marie let out a surprised laugh, her coffee going down the wrong way and causing her to sputter. She coughed and laughed, waving off my alarmed offer of help. I had expected a 'spit take', not a choking incident, and immediately felt guilty. Finally, her belly laugh took over, in an attention-getting way that only she could manage, briefly attracting curious looks from passersby.

"That is *so* you!" she exclaimed between a couple more coughs, wiping tears from her face, clearly not holding a grudge at my timing. I tossed my unruly curls out of my eyes again, thinking as I felt the curls tickle my shoulder that I needed to get a trim soon, and tried to glower in her direction. That just caused her to dissolve once more into laughter.

Finally I conceded the point. "Hence the name," I muttered.

"Well, you did bump into me today," she pointed out.

"What?" I argued. "You bumped into me!"

We both turned in one motion to look to Jim to settle the dispute. He shook his head.

"Leave me out of it," he said, holding up his hands, palms facing us, as though warding us off. "I'm neutral."

"You're supposed to be on my side," I complained.

"I'm always on your side, my sweet klutz," he said, reaching over and squeezing my shoulder affectionately.

"Ugh," Marie groaned. "You two are *still* lovey-dovey?"

"Some things never change," Jim said with warmth, planting a kiss on my cheek for good measure while I smiled sweetly at Marie. "Thirty-four years and still going strong."

Marie sighed and looked at the mulling crowd around us, clearly not willing to get into a relationship discussion.

"Looks like it's almost time for the piping down of the sun," she pointed out. "I assume that's why you're here."

I nodded and held up my camera bag. "I want to get some photos from the bridge," I said.

The bridge over the Penetangore River is the ideal spot to get a shot of the piper at the top of the lighthouse. From the bridge you can see the river flowing out into the lake between two massive concrete piers that form the entrance to the harbour filled with sailboats and other water craft. A glorious sunset reflecting on the water beyond completes the idyllic view.

"Well, you better hurry and get a spot then, before there's no clear shot because of the people in the way," she advised. "Just try not to fall off the bridge," she added teasingly.

I stuck my tongue out at her as I rose from the bench and turned to go, laughing. "See you later?"

"You better."

As we moved away, I noticed a frown on Jim's face. "Sorry that you weren't included in that conversation," I said, misinterpreting his look.

He shook his head. "That's no problem," he answered, clearly distracted.

"What's wrong?"

"I just overheard something a little odd when that piper went by," he explained. "A woman said something about him being treated special, like he's a star, and that he should not be allowed to come back and take a spot whenever he feels like it. Emphasis on the NOT. She sounded really angry."

"Did you recognize her?"

"No," he answered, and then smiled. "It was a weird thing to hear, that's all." He took my hand in his, almost making mine disappear, and we walked together onto the bridge. "I'm sure it doesn't matter. Let's go get your photos."

The Travelling Klutz

So many small towns have unique and quaint traditions. Kincardine is no different, thanks to its strong Scottish heritage. Bagpipes and kilts abound, and the town even has its own registered tartan.

One tradition in town surrounds pipers, the iconic red and white lighthouse, and the stunning sunsets over Lake Huron. In the summer, weather permitting, a piper will climb the 69 steep steps to the top of the picturesque lighthouse and make his or her way outside the lamp room. Once perched outside the eight sided tower, the Phantom Piper, as he or she is called, plays down the sun until it seemingly sinks into the crystal clear waters of the lake. People gather along the beach, on the docks of the harbour, on the bridge crossing the Penetangore River, on the two piers jutting out into the lake, aboard boats, and up at the Queen's Lookout Park to the east, to watch the sun set and to listen to the plaintive tune with which the piper serenades the sun.

Some people often wonder what the fuss is about. The odd few plug their ears or find reason to be far away during the nightly tradition. After all, bagpipe music is not everyone's cup of tea. Or glass of Scotch, if you want to stay with the town's theme.

There is never a lack of people watching the spectacle, however. Maybe they are enjoying the sights and sounds. Or maybe they're waiting to see if this is the night a phantom piper tumbles from that precarious, high up perch, becoming a phantom in truth.

People are funny that way.

Chapter 2

Getting to the spot I wanted on the bridge was easier said than done. The spot was there; perfectly positioned overlooking the river and the lighthouse, beckoning to me in what increasingly seemed to be a sinister way as we struggled through the growing crowd to reach it. The density of the crowd was not the problem. The problem was that many people were recognizing me along the way, and they all wanted to say hello.

It's not that I didn't want to say hello; I just didn't want to do it at that particular moment. I was on a mission.

Having been a reporter in a small town for as long as I had been pretty much guaranteed that I would be recognized. I had interviewed plenty of people in my day. Unfortunately, or fortunately, depending on your perspective, too many for me to recall things like their names and what their story had been. Marie and I had dubbed the phenomenon the Reporter's Curse: the unfortunate side effect of writing everything down. Once the information is written down, you don't have to remember it. You can always check your notes. The reporter's curse was a thing long before the same effect started turning up in regular people, often the younger set, when the internet took the world by storm. Having information at your fingertips has its downside.

The point being, all of the people who stopped me only had one person to remember - me. For me, there were just too many of them to remember. So I didn't even try.

As a result, variations of the same conversation took place over and over as I made my way as fast as I could to the coveted bridge spot.

"Casey! Welcome back," said the anonymous man or woman.

"Thank you so much," I answered non-specifically, while thinking: *I have no idea who you are.*

Them: "What are you doing back in town?"

Me: "I'm writing a travel column and thought this would be a good place to start." *The bridge spot would be a great place to start if I could just get there.*

Them: "I look forward to reading it. Remember when you wrote about ... followed by various old articles that were a highlight to them but one of thousands of articles to me.

Me: "Of course. How could I forget?" *No, not really. Maybe. Vaguely.*

Jim: (Trained years ago to extricate me from such encounters.) "Sorry to interrupt, my sweet, but if you want to get those photos, we should get going."

Me: "You're right." *Thank you Jim! What would I do without you?*

At which point I would reach out to shake a hand or pat a shoulder, smiling at the person because I do actually appreciate that they remember me and my work so fondly.

Me: "Nice to see you again."

Them: "We'll have to catch up later."

But we have already moved on. Once we are out of earshot, Jim invariably asks, "Who was that?" and I shrug, having no answer.

After many such encounters we finally got to the spot I wanted on the bridge. The lighthouse soared tall and proud to our right, its bright white sides and red trim standing out against the cloudless blue sky. In front of us the channel formed by the two concrete piers reached out into the crystalline waters of the lake, a newer but less flashy beacon flashing at the end of the north pier to guide the boats to safe harbour. To our left a number of sailboats bobbed gently in the water of the marina, their masts jutting up into the slowly darkening sky. And behind it all lay the uninterrupted waters of Lake Huron, looking every bit as massive as an ocean, the curvature of the planet actually visible as you scanned the horizon from left to right. The sun was approaching the water, a bright ball of reddish orange, as we took our position.

I pulled my camera out, preparing to take some photos of what was promising to be another stunning sunset. As I did so I nearly elbowed the woman beside me, and then I overcompensated for the near collision and stumbled backwards, stepping onto another person's foot. At the sound of a curse, I turned around, already apologizing.

"I am so sorry," I said, looking up at an older gentleman, who was currently frowning at me. If there could be a human version of Oscar the Grouch from Sesame Street, this elderly man was it. He was on the plump side, with a definite beer belly protruding above the waist band of his rumpled pants. His bushy eyebrows came together above his gray eyes, the bushiness making the frown look more severe. I noticed, however, the numerous laugh lines around his eyes and mouth that belied the grumpy persona he was clearly trying to project, and rather suggested someone who had laughed, and laughed often throughout a long life well lived.

Regardless, he did not appreciate being stepped on.

"I just want to get through this darned crowd and away before that cursed caterwauling starts," he grumbled. "Without," he looked at me pointedly, "getting trampled."

My apology had apparently fallen on deaf ears, which given the fellow's advanced age was a distinct possibility, so I repeated it. Then I got bumped by a fellow klutz passing by and stumbled into him again. He steadied me with a strong grip on my upper arms, then as if remembering he was supposed to be curmudgeonly, pushed me off him.

"You are a menace!" he said, seeming to complain, but now that I was looking for the signs, I could see he was hiding amusement. Before I could say anything else he turned and hurried away, surprisingly spry for a man I guessed might have been around for Confederation. In seconds, he disappeared into the crowd.

"Making new friends I see," Jim teased.

"He said I'm a menace," I pouted.

"Astute," Jim laughed, but upon seeing my pout grow, he pulled me in for a quick hug. "Worry not my sweet," he said. "You may be a menace, but you are my menace."

I giggled and returned his hug. Releasing him, I struggled out of his embrace and turned back to the view of the lake before me.

"I think her name is Suzie," I said out of the blue.

"What?" Jim's clear blue eyes scrunched in confusion.

"That last woman who recognized me," I explained. "Suzie ... something."

"Q?"

"No."

"Homemaker?"

I swatted his arm. "You are not helping. No, not Suzie Homemaker."

"It'll come to you," he assured me. "In the meantime..." He nodded toward the top of the lighthouse, where the piper had just eased his way onto the thin balcony and was getting his pipes into position for his performance.

I took the lens cap off the camera, zoomed in on the piper, and started taking some photos.

"Good, let's get this done then get to the patio for a pint before it gets overrun," I said as I clicked away at the piper and then switched to the increasingly brilliant sunset behind him. I made sure to get photos of both him and the lighthouse in the foreground of the scene, and of the sunset over the water on its own.

"Not a fan?" Jim whispered in my ear from behind me.

"You know I'm not," I said, still taking photos. "Not since that beginner practised his bagpipes in the field behind our house." The sound of that boy and his pipes had haunted my dreams all those years ago and still sometimes did.

"His parents wouldn't let him play the pipes in the house," Jim recalled.

I chuckled at the memory. "Do you blame them? The sound was not only horrendous, but it was loud to boot! The kids thought someone was killing a cat the first time they heard him."

I turned to look back at the town and park high above our position on the bridge and aimed my camera in that direction as the orange of the sunset intensified. I could see the old town hall, positioned high on the hill with its spectacular view of the lake, and the people gathered in the park across the street. The sun was reflecting off the windows of the old rectangular brick building. On a whim, I started taking a few photos of the sun kissed scene.

Suddenly, a loud, quick crack rose above the sound of the pipes. I spun around as the sound of the pipes ended abruptly with a tortured squeal reminiscent of the young piper we had just discussed. The piper atop the lighthouse seemed to freeze for a moment.

Then he tottered and fell off of the balcony to the ground below.

The Travelling Klutz

When we first moved to Kincardine in 1985, Jim had just graduated from the University of Toronto's Mechanical Engineering program. He went to work at the nearby nuclear power plant, where many of the town's residents also worked. At the time, the town's slogan was "Where You're a Stranger Only Once". The basic premise was, and still is, that the people in the small town of 6,000 are, by their very nature, friendly.

And that is a very contagious attitude. People from town always have a smile for those they pass on the street. More often than not you will get a cheerful 'good morning/afternoon/evening' or just 'hello'. If you drop something, someone will pick it up for you. If you are headed into a building, someone is likely to hold the door for you. And almost everyone is willing to answer a question, provide directions, or strike up a conversation - especially if you catch them in a coffee shop.

Having lived right smack dab in downtown Toronto, it was almost an alien concept for us. It took us quite a while to get used to it.

Yes, Kincardine residents are a friendly lot.

Until they're not.

Chapter 3

"What the hell are YOU doing here?" growled a harsh voice behind me.

I turned and felt Jim step up behind me for moral support, resting his hand lightly in the small of my back. I swear I heard him growl back.

"Officer Wolsey," I said, trying to keep the contempt from my voice as I confronted his angry face. I stepped back slightly, as much to take comfort from Jim's presence as to distance myself from the policeman.

He sneered down at me. He had gained some weight since we last met, and while his 6'2" frame concealed it somewhat, I guessed he had to have passed at least 275 pounds. He had never been a small man, and now he dominated all of the space around him. The new weight made his face rounder than ever and it flushed a red that seemed to be getting deeper by the second. I wondered if his colour could be attributed to seeing me again. His hair was now cut close to his head in a style akin to those favoured by army personnel, instead of the messy brown mop I remembered, but that did nothing to disguise the growing amount of gray peppered through it. He was wearing a lightweight tan suit instead of the uniform I was accustomed to seeing him in, but the wrinkled jacket did as little to hide his girth as that uniform ever did.

I straightened to my full height, deciding to not cower in the face of his belligerent attitude. "Did you sleep in that suit?" I asked, ignoring the poke in my back from Jim as I said it.

Wolsey ignored my question. "That is De-tec-tive to you," he barked, accentuating each syllable of the word. I just barely kept myself from jumping at his tone. It wouldn't do to let him think he was intimidating me. Jim's hand rose to squeeze my shoulder. "Why are you at my crime scene?" Wolsey demanded.

I glared into his squinty brown eyes. "De-tec-tive?" I imitated his pronunciation of the word without answering his question. After all, that is technically what he had told me to call him. His eyes narrowed as I said it, giving me a bit of satisfaction. "I wondered why you were in a suit off a Big and Tall Man mannequin instead of a uniform." I delivered the dig and then stood back and watched in fascination, smiling sweetly, as everything from his shoulders up turned redder than the sunset.

Marie took that moment to arrive and interrupt what promised to be a heated exchange. "Tell me you got photos of that!" she exclaimed as she came to a screeching halt beside Wolsey. Only then did she register his looming presence. "De-tec-tive," she said by way of greeting, also sounding out each syllable slowly. Apparently, she'd received the same instruction I had, at some point since his promotion.

He scowled. "I should have known. What are you two up to?"

Jim chose this point to chime in from behind me. "Three," he said calmly.

"What?" Wolsey demanded, looking at my husband as though just noticing that he was there.

"Three," Jim repeated pleasantly. "What are the three of us up to?"

Wolsey looked from one to the other of us, but before he could say anything, a uniformed officer called up to him from the ground below the bridge. The officer stood on the ground between the lighthouse and the river, beside the now covered body of the piper. Wolsey waved a hand to his subordinate, and then turned back to us with a final, scathing look.

"Do NOT go anywhere," he demanded. "All THREE of you." Then he stalked off the bridge toward the stairs. "And do NOT take any more photos!"

Marie snorted. "And do NOT take any more photos," she mimicked. "Get real." She turned to me. "Did you get any?"

I shook my head as I leaned over to take a few of the crime scene from above. Jim nudged me. "Casey!" he admonished.

I looked at him and smiled sheepishly. "Old habits," I said.

Marie cleared her throat, drawing my attention. "Sorry. No photos of his fall," I told her. "I was taking some of the town in the waning light and had my back turned."

Marie sighed in disappointment, but then a smile slowly grew on her lips. "At least you remembered," she said.

"Always look behind you," we both said at the same time.

Marie raised her camera and took a few photos of Wolsey approaching the sad scene below the bridge.

"What did Officer Stick-up-his-butt want?" she asked when she was done.

"That is De-tec-tive Stick-up-his-butt to us," I corrected.

"Well, la-di-da," she quipped. "You can dress up a pig, but he'll still be wallowing in the mud," she groused.

Jim interrupted our laughter, clearly puzzled as to why we found that so funny. "He wasn't happy to see us, or more to the point, her," he said, pointing to me. "He wanted to know why we were here."

Marie shrugged. "I'm sure he did," she said. "He hates the press. He thinks we get in the way. And Casey and I in particular ... riled him up back in the day."

"We wouldn't let him boss us around," I added, giving Marie a warning look. "He didn't take it well."

I could tell Jim suspected there was more to the story than we were telling him, but after a moment of consideration, he just shook his head and let it go. "Well, this ought to be interesting," he mumbled.

It was almost an hour before we saw Detective Wolsey lumber back towards the stairs, and our visions of getting to the pub patio for a beer had vanished. We'd spent the time looking through the photos I'd taken, but had spotted nothing vital at first glance at the tiny camera display. Still, I had pulled out my laptop from my bag and uploaded them in preparation for what I suspected was to come when the detective returned. The computer was now safely stowed in Marie's seemingly bottomless bag. Wolsey came to a stop in front of us, out of breath and red faced.

"Why are you here?" he asked me by way of a greeting. He sounded tired, but I was determined not to feel sorry for him.

"I'm doing a travel column on small, hidden gems of towns in Ontario," I answered.

"And you picked Kincardine?" he growled, unwittingly repeating Marie's earlier question. I chanced a quick wink in her direction.

Wolsey pointed to my camera. "I'm taking that," he stated.

"No, you most definitely are not." I moved it behind my back.

He sighed and ran a hand over his graying hair. "Yes, I am."

"No. You're not," I repeated, glaring at him.

Jim stepped between us. "Surely we can come to an agreement ..." he began.

"I need those photos," Wolsey interrupted him.

"Do you have a warrant?" Marie jumped in, poking the bear.

Wolsey turned suspicious eyes her way. "Were you here at the time?"

"On the bridge or in town?" Marie asked, her eyes dancing mischievously.

"Obviously you were in town," Wolsey snapped.

"Great observation, De-tec-tive," Marie mocked. "Is that why you get paid the big bucks?"

Jim shot her an annoyed look and then tried again with Wolsey. "Detective," he said, ignoring the frowns he got from both me and Marie. "Of course we want to help your investigation any way we can. But Casey is on assignment and needs the camera ..."

"Not my problem," Wolsey interrupted him again.

I could tell my usually even tempered husband was losing his patience, although he was hiding it well. "How about we give you the photo card?" he suggested. "Would that suffice?"

Wolsey looked at him in surprise, clearly not expecting a reasonable person to be anywhere in the vicinity of two women he had long considered to be the bane of his existence. "Well ..." he began.

"There's no warrant," I complained, my voice sounding a lot like a whine even to my own ears, earning a glare from the detective, a decidedly unladylike snort from Marie, and a firm elbow nudge from Jim.

"There's no need," Jim said, shooting me a stern look. He pried the camera from my hands, removed the memory card and handed it to Wolsey. "Here you go sir," he said.

Wolsey looked at the tiny disk in his hand as if it would bite. "Thank you," he finally ground out.

I really thought such a sentence could kill him. You could have knocked me over with a feather.

He turned a less friendly look on me. "Are there any copies?" he snapped.

"What would I copy it to?" I countered, pointing to my open and oddly vacant bag.

He narrowed his eyes, but couldn't come up with a counter argument. Instead he pointed at the three of us before issuing a command. "Stay out of this."

Then he stomped off the way he'd come. We watched him leave, and then Marie and I turned our best innocent gazes at Jim.

He shook his head at both of us. "Yep," he muttered. "This is going to be interesting."

The Travelling Klutz

When you come to visit the Kincardine area, you have a multitude of choices as to where to hang your hat once you get here.

The hotel and motel situation has improved since we first moved to town, with no less than three large chain hotels located out by Highway 21, which skirts the east side of town. There is also another hotel not far from the highway at the north end of town. Each of those is technically within walking distance of downtown. The first three are about a 20 minute walk, with a valley providing a couple of steep hills to traverse en route, while the fourth is a tad bit further away but involves a much gentler walk. Other motels are situated at various spots within the town, with only one right in the core. That one sits kitty-corner to the lighthouse and across from the historic Walker House.

Also right down by the water and very close to the core is a municipally owned trailer park. Those who enjoy camping have other choices outside of town but within a comfortable drive or bicycle ride; two trailer parks to the south and Inverhuron Provincial Park to the north. A bit further away you will also find MacGregor Point Provincial Provincial Park.

Other options include the marina, if you have a boat; one of the numerous bed and breakfasts along the shoreline, or a cottage rental. It all depends on personal preference.

Whichever option you choose, be sure to take care near and around the water and the unfamiliar surroundings. There are many pitfalls about for the klutzy among us.

Chapter 4

After taking our leave of Marie, we walked along the shoreline to our cottage rental in contemplative silence. I have always felt that the strength of relationship can be measured in part by your lack of need to fill every moment with chatter.

Our route took us down Harbour Street to the massive flag pole flying an equally large Canadian flag. The pole is positioned among a cavalcade of colour in a lovely garden, with a path winding past it to the beginning of the north side boardwalk. Of course, it was too dark to see that by the time we strolled past.

I was glad the sun had already set, as I always find it difficult to walk on this boardwalk without looking down at the planks that make it up. A project of the local Lions Club, it was financed by selling boards to individuals and groups whose names were then inscribed onto their board, in return for their donation. I always enjoyed reading who had donated to the project, even though I had gone through, or rather over, each one many times before. Of course, reading the planks at my feet instead of watching where I was going rarely ended well, unless I had someone like Jim to keep me from running into anyone, or from walking off the boardwalk entirely. On this night, in the dark, I was not tempted to read as I walked and we simply enjoyed the stroll.

We proceeded along the shoreline and past Macpherson Park, locally referred to as Tiny Tots Park in reference to the playground nestled in the shade underneath large, old growth trees. The playground equipment had changed significantly over the years, from the bulky and mostly metal contraptions that either scorched the skin on hot days or just generally seemed designed to endanger children's lives, to the brightly coloured plastic units that promised safe play for children of all abilities. In the dusk, the equipment resembled the shadows of hulking giants overlooking the boardwalk.

We passed the Pavilion next - an old concert/dance hall that is now used for all sorts of events throughout the year. On this night its lights were out and the doors were locked. Beyond the heritage building we transferred onto what is locally referred to as Lover's Lane, walking past the rock garden that boasts brilliant flowers and well tended plants on an open piece of land right on the lake. From there it was only a short walk to the rear of the cottage we had rented for the week from a former colleague of Jim's.

We were lucky to get the cottage, as it's not normally rented out. But I guess it's true that it's all in who you know.

We were about to leave the main path onto the trail leading to the cottage when an elderly woman appeared in front of us. Tall and thin with wispy short gray hair, the septuagenarian greeted us with a broad smile. It seemed as though she had been lying in wait.

"Hello there," she said in a strong, steady voice. "I am Mrs. Holmberg. I live year round in this cottage here." She gestured to the cottage next door to the one we had rented. "Are you friends of the Whites?"

"Actually, yes we are," Jim answered her. "I'm Jim Robertson and this is my wife Casey." He put his arms around my shoulders and pulled me in to his side. I put my arm around his waist comfortably. "I worked with Oscar White when we lived here. His family graciously allowed us to rent the cottage while my wife is here writing a travel article for Our Ontario."

Mrs. Holmberg looked at me appraisingly. "And you picked Kincardine?"

Jim snickered. I smiled at the woman, already certain that I liked her. "Nice to meet you," I said, opting to ignore her comment.

"Well, seeing as you're friends of the Whites, I suppose it's all right that you stay here," she said. Her conversational skills certainly jumped around. "Just don't have any wild parties."

"Do we look like party people?" I asked sarcastically.

She took the question seriously. "You never know nowadays." And with that she turned away and disappeared as quickly as she had appeared.

Jim shot me a bemused look as we continued on to the cottage. A humble two bedroom abode, its large pane glass windows faced the lake. The sides were clad with simple brown boards, the style indicating that it had been in the White family for many generations. Beyond the cottage was a hill, upon which was perched a newer garage, with an entrance onto Saugeen Street beyond. Surrounded by tall trees and bushes, the cottage was a bit of lake side seclusion right smack dab in town.

Jim unlocked the door and stood aside. "After you my sweet," he said gallantly.

"Who said chivalry is dead?" I quipped as I went past him into the cottage. To my left was the eat-in kitchen; a large, rectangular wooden table situated right in front of the windows.

To the right was the living room, filled with mismatched furniture that had no doubt been added piecemeal to the cottage when the main home's furniture was updated over the years. The couch looked particularly inviting, overstuffed with dark brown fabric that was worn in places from frequent use. I would have to check it out later, with a good book and a glass of wine. But for now, I walked straight to the kitchen and reached into a cupboard for some glasses. "Wine outside?"

"You read my mind." Jim opened the old gold coloured refrigerator and snagged the one and a half litre bottle of white wine we had put there earlier in the day. We went back outside and settled into two relatively new, heavy plastic Muskoka chairs that were facing the lake.

"I don't suppose I can convince you to stay away from this investigation?" Jim asked after we clinked our glasses in a mini toast and took our first sips of wine.

I looked at him in surprise. "I don't look for these situations, you know."

He laughed. "And yet they seem to find you."

"How about this?" I suggested. "I won't go out of my way to take part in any of this situation."

"So you won't be hanging out with Marie?"

"What? Why would I want to avoid her?"

"Well, she has to investigate as part of her job," he said. "YOUR job is to write about visiting this town, not about a tragic death and the ensuing investigation."

I sighed. "With all that's going on, I'm sure she'll be too busy to hang out," I complained. I took a big drink of wine, and then added, "But she'll want to see my photos from tonight. There might be something she can use."

He sighed. "Fine, we can meet her for breakfast at the coffee shop tomorrow," he said. "But after that, you should really focus on your own work."

"Yes Dad," I teased, rising from my seat to go get my phone. "I'll give her a call and you can get us more wine."

Then I turned and walked right into the picnic table, banging my shin. "Mother Trucker!" I yelped, turning to plop down on the seat I had just slammed into.

"Are you ok?" Jim looked down at me in concern as I rubbed my shin.

"Someone moved the picnic table," I grumbled.

He looked down at the wine glasses in his hands. "Maybe I should cut you off?" he teased.

I frowned at him, and then reached over to snag his phone from his pocket. "By the time you get back I'll have texted Marie and will be waiting back in the comfy chair for my wine."

He turned to go into the cottage, shaking his head the entire way.

The Travelling Klutz

Small towns have all sorts of wonderful spots for friends to gather.

In Kincardine, one such spot is Victoria Park on the north side of the downtown area. With its stately chestnut trees full of blossoms in the spring, attracting squirrels with all of the dropped nuts on the ground in the fall, shading the large expanse of grass divided by a meandering interlocking brick walkway, the park beckons visitors and residents alike. People gather around the tiered water fountain that dates back to Queen Victoria's time; sit on the many benches while their children climb all over the two cannons installed to point out over the lake to protect against potential Fenian raiders from the United States decades before; or take shelter in the large, multi-sided gazebo in the centre.

There is the Lion's Club Splash Pad on Durham Street, where parents can sit on picnic tables or large rock slabs which commemorate the generous donors to the project, and catch up with each other's news while their children cavort in a variety of water features. There is the Off-leash Dog Park, where dog lovers can compare notes while watching their pets run free, contained safely within two acres of fields and woods.

Or there is the quintessentially Canadian spot for gathering, found in every town across the country - the local coffee shop. Kincardine has two of the big chain coffee shops in town, but it is downtown where you will find the best coffee shop. It actually isn't a coffee shop at all but a bakery; a bakery with excellent coffee and plenty of seating.

It's where you can get all of the gossip on recent events with your double-double and complimentary sugar glazed donut.

Where else would one go to get the low down on the death of a piper?

Chapter 5

The following morning, Jim and I made our way on foot to the Best Friends Bakery, located right downtown, where we knew we would find plenty of locals. We took our coffee - a regular blend with milk and half a sugar for me and a dark blend with milk for him - and donuts to a table at the back of the coffee shop. We had been known to enjoy sitting on the stools at a high counter in the front window, watching the people pass by outside, but today we wanted to hear what the locals inside had to say. I also needed room in which to open up my laptop. So we bypassed the window spot, went past the lovely mural of flowers and the sentiment 'A Sweet Friendship Refreshes the Soul' artfully scrawled across the wall by the door, and proceeded to a back table.

All of the tables in the bakery are made of an old farmhouse style door, weathered and rustic, covered with a sheet of glass and set at the perfect height in front of a long bench along the wall. One wall was covered in old barn boards, painted in pastel colours. The benches are old church pews, worn from years of use. The table we sat at had peeling light blue paint and plenty of nicks and scratches. Old, equally weathered wooden chairs lined up along the other side to complete the cozy, farmhouse feel. Light fixtures made from old colanders or coffee cans hung from the ceiling, along with various baking utensils such as sifters and whisks.

"Marie should be here soon," I said as I got out my laptop and set it on the table.

"Good," Jim replied and I looked up in surprise. He smiled and shrugged. "I see a couple of former colleagues over there," he explained, nodding over at a table of four older men that I hadn't noticed when we walked through the front of the bakery. "I thought I'd go and say hello once Marie got here to keep you company."

I studied the table of men. One, I was fairly certain, was the elderly gentleman I had stumbled into on the bridge the night before. Beside him was a stick thin fellow of about 75 years of age, with salt and pepper hair and a beak-like nose that somehow worked for him. In the seats across their table sat two other gentlemen. They looked a little older than us, in their late 60's, and I assumed these were the men with whom Jim was acquainted. The one closest to us reminded me a bit of William Shatner of Star Trek fame, while the one beside him was portly and currently erupting into a belly laugh. It made him look a bit like Santa Claus.

Come to think of it, he really resembled the fellow who played Santa each year for the town's Christmas parade. I should know. I'd taken enough photos of him over the years.

I looked teasingly at my husband. As a reporter, I'd spent a fair amount of time in the town's coffee shops and in this one in particular. I therefore recognized the table, if not the men currently occupying it.

"Since when are your former colleagues members of the ROMEO club?" I asked.

"The ROMEO what now?" Jim looked confused.

"The ROMEO club. That's their table, always has been. The men change over the years, but that table still belongs to the Romeos." I smiled at my stumped hubby, and finally took pity on him. "The acronym stands for Really Old Men Eating Out," I explained.

Jim laughed. "You're making that up," he accused.

I shook my head. "Ask them," I challenged. "And while you are at it..."

"See what they know about the piper," he finished for me. He leaned down and kissed my cheek. "Why do you think I'm going over there?"

I sighed and squeezed his hand. "You're a keeper," I told him.

"And don't you forget it either," he replied, squeezing back and then pulling his hand free.

"Get a room," Marie teased as she approached with her coffee and a muffin. Her donut was in a to-go bag.

Jim chuckled and stepped around her. "I'll just be over there, chatting with the guys," he said.

"You're a little young for the ROMEOs," Marie commented dryly, "but good idea."

Jim turned a bemused look to me before taking his leave.

"So, what do you know?" I asked Marie before she could even sit. "I'm so glad you're not retired yet."

Marie laughed. "Like I will ever be able to retire," she joked, sipping her coffee before settling into her seat.

"So?"

"So. The piper was Matthew Lachlan, 27, single, part of the pipe band for ..." She pulled out her reporter's note book from her bag and flipped through it. "...18 years. He grew up here and was a member of the pipe band from a fairly young age. He lived and worked in Burlington, but still played with the band when he was back visiting his parents." She paused for effect. "Cause of death is unclear until the autopsy comes through."

I frowned. "He fell to his death, right?"

She shrugged and leaned across the table to whisper. "Well, it was either the fall or the gunshot wound to the chest he got before he fell."

I let out a rather loud gasp. A few people turned to look our way and I smiled at them. They quickly looked away.

"Shh!" Marie admonished. "Didn't you notice me whispering that?"

"Sorry," I said sheepishly. "But he was shot? Are you sure?"

"You didn't hear the shot?" Marie asked incredulously. "You were RIGHT THERE."

"I heard something crack. I thought the railing broke," I admitted.

"You, my friend, are out of practice," she teased.

"Dammit Jim," I countered with my best imitation of Bones from Star Trek. "I'm a travel writer, not a crime reporter." The quote must have come to mind because of the ROMEO I thought looked like Shatner. "Do you think many people know?"

"Again. I whispered."

"So that's a no?"

Marie shrugged and peeled the paper off the bottom of her muffin. "If they don't know, they will soon. It's a small town, after all."

I watched her bite into her treat with a look of disgust on my face. "Carrots don't belong in baked goods," I grumbled.

"I'm well aware of your limited palette," she teased. "All the more for me," she said as she took another big bite. She motioned to my laptop. "Anything interesting in your photos?"

"Actually ..." I turned the screen to her so she could see one of the photos I had taken of the old town hall with the sunset reflecting on its brick facade and windows. After what she had just revealed about the cause of the piper's death, I was less confused about what I had captured in the photo, but I wanted her opinion. "Do you see anything odd in this one?"

Marie adjusted the screen to minimize the glare and focussed on the photo. After a few seconds I saw realization dawn on her. She pointed to the spot that had caught my attention last night.

"What is that?"

"Well, I thought it was just a weird glare, but given your new information," I whispered, "I would have to say that I caught a picture of the muzzle flash from a gun, up in the window of the old town hall."

Jim joined us with new coffees shortly after that stunning revelation.

"So, what did you find out?" I asked, saluting him with my fresh cup of coffee in gratitude.

"Oh, you know," Jim drawled. "The piper's name, who knew him ... and the fact that he was shot."

"How do they know that already?" Marie demanded, looking over at the ROMEOs in surprise. "The press release came out just seconds before I came here!"

Jim shrugged. "Small town," he mumbled around a mouth full of apple fritter.

I frowned."You got another donut?" I reached over and patted his belly. "Are you sure you need that?" His belly was really fine, but I saw no reason to pass up an opportunity to tease him.

"About as much as you need this," he countered, producing a white bag I hadn't noticed. I grabbed it and happily pulled out a vanilla cupcake.

"My favourite," I said, taking a big bite of the butter cream icing.

Marie cleared her throat.

"What?" Jim asked. "You still have your donut and haven't even finished your muffin."

I decided to break it up before there was a food fight. I turned the computer screen to him and watched as he quickly saw what we had already noticed.

"Wow, that was quite a shot!" he exclaimed, staring at the photo. He looked at Marie. "Who in town can make a shot like that?"

"A really good photographer?" I deadpanned before she could answer.

"I meant the actual shot, from the gun, not the photo."

Marie ignored that exchange, swallowed the last bite of her carrot muffin and washed it down with a swig of coffee. "Any number of people," she answered. "It could be one of the members of the Nimrod Gun Club, or any one of the hunters in the area."

"It would likely be easier to make a list of people who DON'T know how to shoot guns," I pointed out. "So let's change our focus. Why would someone want young Mr. Lachlan dead? He didn't even live here. Was he into anything bad or weird? Was he hated by anyone?"

Jim shook his head. "Not according to the fellows over there," he said. "And they seem to know everything." He looked pointedly at Marie. "Maybe you should hire them."

"I don't need a gossip column," she grumbled.

"Anyway, they said Lachlan was popular. He was even a Big Brother to a fatherless kid when he was little more than a kid himself. Plus he volunteered regularly at different events, both before he left for school and whenever he was in town."

"That makes no sense. Maybe he broke someone's heart." I rubbed my forehead as I thought. "Hey, remember that woman at the bridge last night?"

"There were a lot of women on the bridge last night," Jim pointed out dryly. "Including the two of you. Can you be more specific?"

"The one you heard bad-mouthing the piper," I reminded him.

"Oh yeah," he said. "She said he wasn't that special."

"What did she look like?" Marie asked.

"I don't know. Shorter than Casey ..."

"That narrows it down," Marie muttered dryly.

I rolled my eyes at her reference to what she always called my freakish height. "My height comes in handy. I can see over top of lots of people. I help old ladies in the grocery store reach things on the top shelf."

"... kind of plain, nothing that really stood out," Jim continued, ignoring our little detour.

"He doesn't really check out other women," I bragged to Marie.

Jim shook his head at me in exasperation. After a moment, he asked, "What about that guy you bumped into? He didn't seem to like pipers and was in a big hurry."

"We don't really like pipers, but we wouldn't shoot one," I pointed out. "Besides, you just spoke to him. Did he seem guilty to you?"

Jim looked over at the ROMEO table in surprise. "Norm?" he asked. "Gosh, I didn't recognize him!" He shook his head. "No, he definitely didn't seem guilty to me."

"That and I seriously doubt that he could have made it up to the old town hall, after we saw him, in time to make that shot," I added. I turned to Marie. "Anything to add to the conversation?" I asked teasingly.

But she was ignoring me and staring in the direction of the entrance. I looked that way and saw a very angry looking detective headed our way.

"Ah, crap on a cracker," I grumbled.

The Travelling Klutz

Kincardine's old town hall sits perched at the highest point of downtown, at the south end of the commercial area. Built in 1872, it is an example of Italianate style; the hall consists of a rectangular, beige building with two floors and an attic. The town bell, which once resided in a cupola on the roof, is now displayed in front of the building at ground level. Restored in 2011 and renamed the Kincardine Centre for the Arts, the bottom floor currently houses an art gallery and photographic museum where the town council chambers and offices used to be. Upstairs is a hall, complete with stage, which now supports both an amateur and professional theatre.

The building is flanked by Victoria Park to the east and Queen's Lookout Park to the west. Like the western park, the old town hall has a stunning view overlooking the lake, harbour, and lighthouse below from its many front windows.

When opening an old, heavy door, such as the one leading to the upstairs theatre, remember to stand to the side of the opening, or you are apt to get a door in the face. Especially if the person leaving the building is in a hurry.

Chapter 6

The unexpected run-in with the Kincardine area's newest detective went about as expected.

"I thought I would find you here," he grumbled.

Marie held up her phone for all to see. "You asked my staff where to find me," she stated tersely. "Did you think they wouldn't warn me?"

Wolsey ignored her and turned to me. "I wanted to return this," he said, tossing my camera memory card down on the table in front of me.

That was when he saw the photos on my computer.

"Bloody hell! You told me you had no copies," he snarled.

"Actually, De-tec-tive, I believe I asked you what I would copy the memory card to," I replied. "Not once did I say I didn't do it."

"Delete those."

"Let me think. No."

His eyes narrowed. He was about to say something when his phone chimed. He glared at us and looked at the text he had received.

"I have to go."

"And we were just starting to get along," Marie muttered.

He turned his glare on her. "Stay out of this case. I don't want to warn you again."

"And yet I have a feeling this won't be the last time," Jim lamented.

As Wolsey headed for the door, Marie called after him. "Did the autopsy results come in?"

Every head in the place turned to look at him. With one last glare in our direction, he stormed off in a huff.

I waited until he was gone before turning to Marie. "Who do we talk to about getting into the theatre?" I asked.

She smiled, looking every bit the part of the cat that ate the canary. "Funny you should ask," she said, digging in her voluminous bag and coming up a few seconds later with a set of keys. "I just so happen to still have the keys the Bluewater Summer Playhouse president gave me when I was doing last week's story on the renovations up there." She dangled them and they jingled cheerfully. "I haven't had a chance to return them yet."

"Great," Jim drawled under his breath. When I looked pointedly at him, he concentrated on finishing his coffee.

"Well, what are we waiting for?" I got to my feet and gathered my garbage to toss into the bin on my way out. "Let's go!"

We went to the door located by the ground mounted historic town hall bell. The entire building was designated as historically significant, something I was certain had saved the big, plain, rectangular box from being torn down many times over. It certainly wasn't because of its beauty, as far as I was concerned.

Marie was about to unlock the door when it burst open from the inside. She, being nearer to the side of the door with the opening, was able to jump clear. That, of course, left me right in the way of the heavy vintage fire door and it rammed into me. I was knocked backwards and fell flat onto my butt.

As Jim, who had been following us rather unenthusiastically a few steps behind, rushed to my side, we heard a frazzled "Sorry", followed by a slightly panicked "Out of my way". I looked up in time to see a woman rush by in a blur of dark hair and tartan. I saw Jim pause slightly before reaching down to help me up.

"Are you ok?" he asked, concern showing in his blue eyes. I hazarded a glance at Marie from my spot on the pavement, and she seemed to be making a valiant effort not to laugh.

"Just embarrassed," I mumbled, accepting his helping hand and getting cautiously to my feet. I rubbed my behind and winced. "That's going to bruise," I muttered. "What was that anyway? The Tasmanian devil?"

"You think the Tasmanian devil would apologize?" Marie asked. "Not very devilish."

Jim sighed. "I'm not sure," he admitted, letting the sentence hang as though he had more to add.

I looked at him expectantly. "But...?" I drew out the word.

He sighed. "You know me so well," he said. "The voice was familiar somehow." At my raised eyebrows, he added, "Give me time, I'll remember why."

I nodded and we cautiously opened the door, peeking around it to make sure no one else was bursting out of the building. There was no one there, which left us with a clear view of the long, wide staircase leading to the second floor.

"I thought no one was supposed to be here," I stated the obvious.

"There wasn't supposed to be anyone here," Marie answered as she reached the top of the stairs and turned right to enter the theatre. She stopped so fast that I ran right into her, almost falling for the second time of the day. The only good thing about that was that I would have taken her down with me. And hopefully used her to break my fall.

She gave me an irritated look before she pushed me away and stepped aside. What I saw took my breath away.

Every table and chair in the hall had been shoved to the side or upended as though someone had been trying to ransack the place. The phrase 'no stone unturned' came to mind.

Jim came around the corner and stared. "Are these the renovations you mentioned?" he quipped.

"No."

"Are you sure?"

"I'm positive." Marie turned her irritated glare on him. I was just glad to be out of the line of fire.

"Well, I'm not taking any photos up here for my article," I muttered, moving into the room.

"Don't touch anything," Marie cautioned. "We're going to have to call the cops."

"Must we?" I whined. I really didn't want another encounter with local law enforcement.

"Yes. But, we can look around first," Marie smiled. "Cautiously, of course."

"Of course," I agreed.

Jim shook his head. "I think I'll stay back here where it's safe, if it's all the same to you two."

"Chicken," I tossed over my shoulder as I moved further into the room. "Don't forget I got bowled over by a door outside."

Jim ignored me.

Marie and I weaved around the furniture, looking for anything out of place among the already seriously out of place furniture. I wandered over to the westward facing wall of windows to check out the view. I could see the lake in all its glorious blue splendour, the lighthouse, and the tops of sailboats from this spot. I looked down and frowned.

"Look at this," I called out to the other two.

They both joined me and I smirked at Jim, who ignored my look. All three of us looked at the small hole at the bottom of the far left window. In front of it was a table, and clearly visible in the dust on that table were three spots arranged in a perfect triangle where something had recently rested.

"Do those look like marks that tripod legs would leave to you guys?" I asked as I took a photo of the table.

Marie nodded."Like for a camera. Or for a gun," she said, pulling out her phone to call the police.

I leaned over to look under the table. The floor looked as though it had been swiped clean, like someone had felt around underneath, looking for something.

"What do you think she was looking for?" I wondered aloud.

"Evidence," Marie grunted as she bent over to look under the table as well. "Like a discarded shell maybe?"

We straightened and Jim and I wove our way carefully back towards the stairs. As we retreated, Marie was reporting what we assumed to be a break-in to the police. Soon she joined us at the top of the stairs.

"They said to wait outside," she told us.

We trudged back down the stairs and out the door, opening it carefully in case someone as unlucky as I was happened to be on the other side.

"Did you recognize the woman at the door?" I asked Marie.

"I was too busy watching you fall on your butt," she laughed. "She had dark hair."

"And she seemed to have a beef with Lachlan," Jim added.

We looked at him in shock, prompting a bemused smile from him. "I remembered where I'd heard her voice. She was the woman from last night, the one on the bridge who was complaining about the piper."

"How is it that you keep turning up at my crime scenes?" a scowling Detective Wolsey asked, glaring at each of the three of us in succession. He looked like he had slept in his black, non-descript four-door sedan. When he got out of the vehicle, a fast food bag was swept out of it with him and blew down the street like tumbleweed made of restaurant trash. *So he eats in the vehicle too*, I thought.

Jim glared at Marie and me both, daring us to take the bait. Instead of commenting on the condition of his suit or his car, we followed him up to the auditorium to show him what we had found.

"Now that is hardly fair De-tec-tive," I complained, unable to stay silent for long. "We were at the last crime scene the same way two thirds of the people in town were there."

"We were more overlooking it, really," Marie added.

In my peripheral vision I saw Jim back up a few steps. The traitor. Then again, you never know when you will need someone to bail you out of jail.

Wolsey was getting red under the collar. Literally. "What were you doing here?" he demanded.

"Ah, well, I wanted to get pictures of the theatre for my article," I began.

"And I had the key," Marie added.

I nodded. "And I also wanted photos of the view from this building ..."

"You expect me to believe you need so many photos for ONE article?" Wolsey barked incredulously.

"Have you seen Our Ontario magazine?" I answered his question with one of my own. After all, the tactic had worked many times before. "It's a glossy publication that uses many, high-quality, colour photographs. It's not a newspaper." I turned to Marie. "No offense."

She frowned. "Some taken."

"I didn't mean ..."

She waved her hand at me. "Whatever," she grumbled.

The redness had spread up to the detective's cheeks.

"OK, fine. You broke in for pictures..."

"I had the key," Marie sing-songed the earlier bit of information that Wolsey had clearly chosen to ignore. She dangled them in his face, the jingle sounding somewhat sinister this time. "We did NOT break in."

He backed away from her a step but otherwise ignored her and continued speaking. "...and you came up here. Then what happened?"

"We found it like this." I swept an arm out and around in my best Vanna White imitation, causing Jim to jump back even further.

"Did you touch anything?

"Honestly, De-tec-tive," Marie drawled. "This isn't our first rodeo."

"Or crime scene," I added.

"This week," I heard Jim mumble behind me.

The redness had reached Wolsey's hairline. I think there may have been some steam coming out of his ears. Or maybe that was sweat evaporating from the heat. Either way.

"Did you see anyone?" Wolsey asked through a clenched jaw.

"Well, actually..." I began.

"There was that woman," Marie added.

"She knocked me down." I tried my best to look affronted.

"Right on her butt," Marie supplied, chuckling.

Wolsey was looking from one to the other of us like he was watching a tennis match.

"Down at the front door," I concluded, nodding towards the stairs.

Wolsey looked over at Jim, who nodded and mumbled, "You can't make this stuff up."

The detective levelled us with a glare. "These two might." With a put upon sigh, he jotted down some notes in his black note book. "You couldn't have led with this?" he asked.

"I kind of forgot for a bit," Marie ventured.

"I didn't," I said, rubbing my bruised behind.

The detective ignored me. "What did she look like?"

"Kind of funny, landing on her butt like that," Marie deadpanned.

Wolsey ran a hand over his head, looking like he would pull his hair out, if it were long enough for him to get hold of. I took pity on him. Kind of.

"She hit me with a door," I pointed out. "I didn't get a chance to check her out."

Wolsey harrumphed, jotted something down in the book, and then turned to Marie.

"She just ran past us so fast. She had dark hair," she offered. "Average height?"

Wolsey wrote that down and turned to Jim next.

"I was worried about Casey and didn't notice much," he said. "But she was wearing a kilt, I think."

"That narrows it down," I grumbled.

"And she apologized," Jim added, sending me a quick shut-up frown. "I think I recognized her voice."

Wolsey looked about ready to explode. I wondered briefly how we would explain bits of detective to the next one who turned up.

"You couldn't have led with THAT?" He was very close to full-out yelling.

"Recognized is the wrong word Detective. I apologize," Jim said quickly. "I meant that I had heard that voice before."

Wolsey took a deep, calming breath before asking, "Where and when did you hear it?"

"Last night, in the crowd by the lighthouse, about a half hour before the shooting."

Wolsey jotted that down in the book. "And what did she say then?"

"She said something about the piper going into the lighthouse not deserving the special treatment," Jim answered.

"Anything else?"

"No sir, not that I can remember." Jim had an exaggerated respect for police, if you ask me.

"Alright." Wolsey started to close his note book, but hesitated. "Did you see anything else once you got up here?" He almost seemed to be cringing in anticipation of the answer.

"Well, actually..." I began.

He levelled me with a cold stare and I squirmed a bit, but just on the inside so he wouldn't know I was nervous.

"...I went to take a photo of the view, to give the magazine a lot of choices..."

"Without touching anything," Marie added.

"Right. And I noticed a little hole in the far window."

"And a table in front don't forget," Marie supplied helpfully.

"Yes, with a table in front of it. And on the table are weird marks in the dust..."

"Like a tripod might make," Marie added.

"But not mine!" I was quick to clarify. "I didn't bring mine with me."

Then we both turned our best innocent looks on him again. "And that's all," we declared in unison.

There was silence for so long I thought we may have caused the good detective to go into shock. Finally, he lifted his arm and pointed to the exit, reminding me of the Ghost of Christmas Past from *A Christmas Carol*. You know, if the ghost were massively hulking and grouchy.

Jim had been in that play, in this very theatre.

"Get away from my crime scene," Wolsey growled.

We wasted no time doing just that. As we scrambled down the stairs he called out after us. "And do NOT leave town."

The Travelling Klutz

The town of Kincardine is much more than just a haven for all things Scottish. It's a paradise for walkers and hikers.

For instance, the downtown core is within walking distance of the beaches and harbour, and very pleasant to stroll through. There are many unique shops and boutiques, gift shops and sport stores, cafes and restaurants. You will find all of this in buildings whose original architecture and charm, inside and out, has been lovingly maintained.

From many locations throughout town you can access an incredible network of trails. The trails link the boardwalk along the shores of Lake Huron to the Labyrinth Peace Garden off Queen Street, onto the numerous forested and river side trails that wind throughout the Penetangore River valley and beyond. Stretching for 22 kilometres, the all season trails make it easy to forget that you are anywhere near civilization at all, when in fact you are just minutes away. You can leave your troubles behind, if just for a while.

It is not difficult at all to spend an entire day exploring the trails, so pack some water and snacks, grab your walking stick and hiking shoes, and don't forget your camera for when you come *across the 'face tree', the knots of which form a distinctive looking face that seems to watch you as you walk past.*

For those klutzes among you, remember to watch your step. While many of the trails and bridges, both permanent and temporary, are impeccably groomed by dedicated volunteers, there can be spots where you can lose your footing. Especially when the ground is wet following a rainfall, or in the fall with the increased litter of falling leaves.

You just never know what you might stumble across.

Chapter 7

We'd had our fill of crowds in general, or as I had heard them described by some locals, city-ots (sounding like idiots), referring to how difficult some visitors can be. I suppose we fell into that category, now that we had moved away and returned to visit. I had also had my fill of police encounters. We therefore decided to venture onto the town's extensive trail system for some recharging in nature. I wanted some photos of the locally famous 'Face Tree' and some of the more idyllic spots to be found along the wooded banks of the Penetangore River.

Disregarding the inherent danger of me hiking on trails when it had rained a bit over night, we donned our hiking shoes, filled our water bottles, and headed for the Queen Street entrance to the trails. We walked quickly past the Labyrinth Peace Garden, where a few people strolled about quietly among the stones and numerous different plants, contemplating whatever they wished in peace. I was not feeling very contemplative myself, so we skipped the garden and headed towards the woods. We could hear the river off to our right as we walked down a wide walkway, which gradually narrowed as the maple, pine, ash, spruce, and birch trees closed in from both sides. As soon as the trees completely closed around us and the trail narrowed down to a width that fit no more than two people, we both sighed in relief.

"What a couple of days," Jim stated the obvious.

I nodded. "Who would have thought a simple travel article could lead to such chaos?"

Jim lifted an eyebrow and gave me a bemused look.

I chuckled. "Okay, point taken, but it has been years since I have gotten mixed up in..." I fell silent, searching for the right word.

"Shenanigans?" Jim offered.

"Troubles," I countered.

"Disorder."

"Difficulties."

"Turbulence."

"I'm not an airplane! Agitation."

"What are you, a washing machine? Excitement."

"Violence," I said sadly.

"Turmoil," he countered.

I sighed. "All of those things. I would go on but I find myself sans, without, bereft of a thesaurus."

Jim smiled, coming to a stop and pulling me into a hug. "It may have been years since you've had this kind of thing happen," he said, "but there seems to be a De-tec-tive who has a good memory." He paused. "What did the two of you do to him anyway?"

"Why do you assume WE did something to HIM?" I demanded, getting an exasperated look in response. I pried myself out of his arms and headed down the path.

"Fine, be that way," he said. "But you know you'll tell me the root of all of this someday," he called after me.

We walked in silence for a while, listening to the bubbling sound of the river get louder as the trail slowly headed towards it.

"Marie seems to have represented us well since I've been gone," I said after a few more minutes of silence.

"You two shouldn't push him so much," Jim warned.

"We can't help it," I told him. "It's just so much fun!"

He shook his head as we stopped to watch the water flow past us. "If you get arrested, you can spend a night in jail before I come bail you out. It seems that would be the only way for me to get some peace when the two of you are together."

I moved to slap his shoulder, but he lunged to one side to avoid the 'love tap'. His attempt to avoid me nearly sent him tumbling down the muddy bank of the river, but he regained his footing at the last minute.

"Who's the klutz now?" I teased.

We turned away from the water and continued down the path in companionable silence. I uncapped my bottle and was taking a sip of water when Jim spoke.

"For a bit, I thought Marie could have been the killer."

I spat water out in shock. "What? Why on earth would you think that?"

He shrugged, and began ticking off reasons as he raised one finger at a time. "Newspapers are dying. The shooting is a big story. She was the only reporter there." He gave me a pointed look over three upright fingers. "Her story was picked up by the nationals, was it not?"

I frowned. "Setting aside that you think one of my oldest friends could be a murderer, you are forgetting one important thing."

"No, I'm not," he countered. "I said that I thought so at first. But she reached our position on the bridge far too fast after the shooting. I know she's been training for a triathlon, but she couldn't have made it from upstairs in the old town hall down to the bridge that quickly."

"Glad to hear it," I grumbled. We were quiet for a while as I stewed about how he could have thought Marie was a suspect. Finally, I asked, "But who could it be?"

"Well," Jim speculated as we came to one of the permanent bridges that had been installed over the river. We walked to the centre and stopped, leaning on the railing and watching the water pass by under our feet. "Isn't it usually someone close to the victim?"

"I heard that he wasn't married and that he has had the same girlfriend for years," I said. "He volunteered with the public. They are a notoriously unpredictable lot. Maybe he upset someone."

Jim shook his head. "The ROMEOs," he used air quotes as he said the group's name, "said the guy was universally liked. A piper, a volunteer, he was an all around upstanding member of the community who will be missed. Everyone was glad to see him during his return visits home."

I frowned. "Well that woman certainly didn't seem to be glad to see him."

"No, she didn't. I wish we knew who she is."

"We seem to be running into her a lot," I said as I took some scenic photos. I zoomed in on a shape down the river a bit and realized it was a crane - the bird, not the construction machine. It was standing in the river, its feathers shining in the sunlight. I quickly snapped some photos before it flew away, even getting one of it in flight just above the water. "We'll have to keep a look out for her." I brought the last photo up on the camera's screen and turned it to show Jim.

"Nice," he said. We moved back from the railing and headed back to the path from which we'd come. "Who knows, maybe it isn't personal at all," he suggested. "There was Norm, the older guy who hates all things pipe and drums."

I made a face. "Your new ROMEO buddy? I thought you liked him."

"I do, but that doesn't mean he can't be a suspect."

"If Marie couldn't reasonably make it back to the bridge in time, there's no way he could have made it from where I bumped into him on the bridge to the old town hall in time to make that shot."

"True," Jim conceded. "But there may be others who aren't fond of pipers."

"We're not fans," I offered, heading towards a side trail that forked off to the left and would lead to the area where the 'Face Tree' was located.

"Well, we weren't involved," he began before my startled cry stopped him.

As I headed down a small hill, my left foot slid out from under me. My right leg, not remotely moving yet, bent under and behind me much further than it has in years as I crashed down onto it, causing a searing pain in my knee. I automatically rolled to my left, landing on my hip with a jarring impact, grasping for any purchase to help relieve the pressure on my knee. My hand found a large stick in the mud and I pulled on it, hoping to steady myself in order to straighten the right leg, which was still shooting lightning pain throughout my body.

Yes, really, I grabbed a stick in the mud. Or at least that's what I thought I'd grabbed. I continued to slide down the muddy incline, finally coming to rest halfway down. I was covered in mud from shoulders to feet, both on my side and my back. I held onto the stick like my life depended on it, even though I was disgusted that it hadn't been of more use.

Jim rushed to my side, easily leaping down the hill and turning to face me. "Are you okay? Don't move! Can you get up?"

"Which?" I snapped. "Don't move or get up?"

Jim didn't answer immediately and I was perturbed that I was not garnering more attention from him. After all, I was in pain! With a loud groan, I glanced up to see why he was no longer expressing concern for my well being.

"How about you let go of that first and then I'll help you up," he said, his voice full of trepidation.

Confused, I turned to look at the stick and yelped in surprise. I dropped it and slid down the rest of the hill on my butt towards him. When he offered me his hand, I let him slowly pull me to my feet.

Because what I'd grabbed was not a stick at all. What I'd grabbed was a rifle.

"Well, son of a witch," I stammered, shifting to stand on one foot and experimenting with bending my right knee. I groaned in pain.

Jim sighed and pulled out his cell phone.

"Wolsey is going to love this," he grumbled.

I eased myself down onto a nearby rock with a moan and made a call of my own, to give Marie a heads up. This was definitely getting more interesting by the minute.

The Travelling Klutz

There's an urban legend, old wives' tale, or whatever you would like to call it, circulating among the residents of the town of Kincardine.

The claim, and no one dares to actually check because they don't want it to be untrue, is that National Geographic magazine called the sunsets on the shores of this small town the most beautiful in Canada. It is a heady claim, to be sure, and if you have never visited the town in the summer, you are likely to scoff at the notion. Most likely you believe, as all of us do, the sunsets wherever you live to be the most magnificent in the country.

Once you visit the town and go down to any of its beaches at sunset, you will give more credence to the claim. You look out at the vast expanse of sparkling blue water, and it will remind you of the Caribbean Sea. When you sit on the beach, or better yet, share a big blue beach chair with friends or a loved one, and watch the sun sink into the horizon, you will give yourself over to the 'best sunsets in the country' line of thought. It is truly an awe inspiring sight. And Kincardine's beaches are an excellent site from which to enjoy that sight.

Just be careful on those giant chairs. They're called big for a reason and are quite high up. If you fall off one, you might miss a critical moment in whatever action is going on around you.

Chapter 8

This time the interaction with the police was surprisingly, even a bit disappointedly, uneventful. That was due in large part to Detective Wolsey's absence. Even he gets to take a day off, apparently.

It was actually a relief to skip the traditional detective baiting. I was quite sore from my fall and had still to hike back out to our starting point at the Labyrinth. I was covered in mud that was now drying and caking on my skin, making it as itchy as it was embarrassing. It did have the unintended benefit of protecting me from mosquitoes as we waited for the police to tell us we could leave. I am nothing, if not a glass half full woman.

When I'd called to give Marie a heads-up, I also arranged for her to meet us at Geddes Park to give us a ride to the cottage. Or to the hospital, depending on how I felt after the hike back to civilization.

"What were you doing, mud wrestling again?" Marie asked, taking in my appearance with a mischievous smirk.

Jim did not miss the look I gave her, begging her to keep quiet, but he only raised an eyebrow at me. I sighed in relief, not wanting to go into an explanation of our history with mud wrestling at the moment. Or ever.

"Ask me tomorrow," I mumbled to Jim and hoping he'd forget, while shooting her another warning glance. We walked over to her car, a simple silver Ford Focus sedan, and Jim opened the front door for me. Marie had lined the seat and back with towels to protect the upholstery. I eased myself into the seat, careful not to disturb the towels. Once she and Jim were in the car, I launched into a detailed explanation of what I had inadvertently discovered and of our interaction with the police.

"It was basically civil," I concluded.

"Well that's disappointing," she observed.

"It was a nice change, actually."

"So, do they think it was THE rifle?" she asked.

"All I got when I asked was 'We cannot comment on that ma'am'."

Marie snorted. "Sounds like a yes to me. Why else would someone dump it in the woods? Those things are expensive." She glanced over at me as she stopped at one of the three stop lights in the downtown area. "You also got photos, right?"

"Yes," I snapped. "I took them to distract me from the pain I was in."

"Sorry," she said, immediately contrite. "That was inconsiderate of me."

"She did take pictures," Jim piped up from the back seat. "I couldn't convince her to take it easy."

She smiled at me fondly. "Always the reporter." She turned onto Saugeen Street and headed to the cottage.

I smiled back. "I learned from the best."

"Sorry to break up this mutual admiration society," Jim teased, "but did you have any luck finding out who owns rifles in town, Marie?"

She shook her head. "I went to the Nimrod Club," she said, referring to the local shooting range south of town. "They said not all rifle owners are members. At this point a list of people who don't own rifles would actually be easier and shorter to make. Just like Casey said earlier." She pulled into the driveway of our cottage and stopped the car.

I sighed. Jim was already out of the car and opening my door.

"Do you need help?" Marie asked. She got out and stood with the driver's side door open, leaning on the roof of the car and looking across it at the two of us.

Jim shook his head. "That's what I'm for," he said, "Picking her up and cleaning up the mess."

"My Prince Charming," I purred, patting his arm as I hobbled away from the car with his support.

Marie shook her head in mock disgust. "Are we still on for sunset at the beach?" she called after us.

"Unless you hear from me saying I've relocated to the hospital, we'll be there," I answered. "First one there grabs a spot on a big chair!"

As I hobbled with Jim's help towards the stairs leading down to the cottage, Mrs. Holmberg appeared behind us.

"What happened to you?" she asked, looking distastefully at my mud covered clothes.

"Casey took a spill," Jim answered her. I'm sure he followed that up with the word 'again' under his breath.

"Into a pig sty?" The old woman laughed at her own joke. For my part, I failed to see the humour. Maybe I'd appreciate it tomorrow.

"I just fell down on a muddy trail," I explained, turning back to the stairs in a not so subtle hint.

"Well you go get cleaned up dear," she advised, "and I'm sure you will feel much better."

I turned around to say thank you, but she had already returned to her property. Either I was getting slow or Mrs. Holmberg was a retired ninja.

I had a long shower to get the mud off me, and then filled the tub with hot water, adding a splash of bubble bath for a soak that I hoped would relieve my rapidly stiffening muscles. I was discovering muscles I'd never noticed before thanks to all of my recent mishaps.

"You have to stop doing this kind of stuff, my sweet." Jim eerily echoed my own thoughts on the matter. He handed me a glass of white wine to sip on while I relaxed.

"I'm so lucky to have you," I said and took a good, long swig of wine. I sighed and leaned back in the tub. "Thank you." I looked up at him sheepishly. "It's not like I do it on purpose," I protested.

"Sometimes I wonder," he mumbled.

"What was that?"

"I just said how sexy you look all strategically covered in bubbles," he said, laughing when I raised my eye brows in response. "You take your time, and then we'll go have a nice l'upper," he said, referring to our term for a meal that was a combination of a late lunch and an early supper.

"Sounds good," I called after him as he left, closing the door behind him.

I must have dozed off: the combination of wine, warm water and bubbles, and soothed aches acting as a soporific. Soon I was deep in dream land. I dreamed I was dressed as a piper, complete with a kilt of Kincardine tartan and bagpipes. Which was likely enough of a nightmare, for me and anyone who would have to listen to my lack of musical talent. But it got worse. In the dream I was walking along Harbour Street towards the lake and was completely alone. In a very uncharacteristic detail, the street was deserted. As I reached the small fountain between a heritage apartment building and the Erie Belle restaurant, I heard footsteps behind me, but in the twilight I couldn't make out more than a shadowy figure when I turned to look behind me.

"Don't go up into the lighthouse," a woman yelled at me. "You don't deserve the honour of piping down the sun."

I was overcome with chills and quickened my step. My eye was then drawn to a shadowy figure ahead to my right. I started to cross to the opposite side of the street.

"Why can't you people give it a rest?" a man yelled at me. "Even God rested one day a week."

I ignored him and tried to go faster, heading to the lighthouse. Another shadow popped up in front of me and I heard a sinister whisper as I hurried past.

"Keep going. We can use another juicy news story."

I jolted awake with a yelp, sloshing the now cool water over the side of the tub, soaking the floor. Jim rushed into the room and stepped in the water, soaking his socks.

"I can't even leave you to relax in a bath!" he complained, dropping a towel onto the floor to sop up the spill.

"I dreamed I was a piper and shadow people were stalking me," I explained as I got out of the tub with a wince. He wrapped me in a towel and hugged me gently, shaking his head and chuckling.

We headed to the patio at Gilley's Feedlot, our favourite place in town to have a pint when we were residents. The patio is a long rectangle, between the restaurant and the building next door, with a huge maple tree in the centre. The tree's branches reach high above the patio and provide shade, with the help of smaller vegetation and table umbrellas, making the patio a small oasis. We selected a table a few spots away from the entrance, where we could watch the people going by but they couldn't see our table nearly as well.

My knee was very stiff and sore, making me lean heavily on Jim's arm as we walked to the table and settled in for l'upper. We each ordered a pint of beer and food, and then sat in companionable silence while waiting for our meal to arrive. It was not long before we picked up snippets of conversations from the tables nearby.

"They charged him a thousand dollars!" a slim, red haired woman said between sips of white wine. She was speaking to a short, portly woman with close cropped dark hair. "I heard that he was late paying the bill."

"I heard that he hates those slogans the pipe band came up with," a younger man to our right was telling the pretty blonde at the table with him. "He said that 'Trust us, it's big' is lewd and 'Pants Optional' encourages immorality."

I looked at Jim and mouthed "I wonder who?"

Jim shrugged and had a drink of his beer.

"She's a new piper," a middle-aged man with graying hair at a table across from us said. "She thinks she's better than she really is." The woman with him, whose hair was clearly coloured as it did not seem to match the aged look of the rest of her, nodded sagely.

"I heard he was having a fling, with a married woman!" the companion of the first woman said in a shocked tone of voice.

"Here's your prime rib." The waiter startled us out of our eavesdropping as he placed the meal of beef, Yorkshire pudding, rice, and mixed vegetables in front of Jim. "And your chicken fingers," he added, placing the basket filled with chicken fingers and fries in front of me. Jim took the Yorkshire pudding off his plate and transferred it to mine and I smiled in thanks. We ordered another pint of beer each and dug in.

After l'upper we drove down to Station Beach, a route we would normally have opted to walk, but even with the extra pint of beer I had enjoyed, my knee protested at the very thought. The rest at the patio seemed to have had the opposite effect that I'd hoped and the muscles had seized up on me.

The beach was getting crowded with people. Since it was a hot night, still well above 25°C, quite a few people were frolicking in the water. Others were sprawled on towels and blankets on the sand. Over at the piers, you could see numerous people strolling up and down the structure, and some fishing over the side.

Out in the water a number of boats bobbed in the light waves and a Sea-Doo zipped by, creating a wake for some kids to jump into a little while later.

I turned towards our destination. It was all I could manage to hobble from the parking lot, over the boardwalk, and through the sand to a big blue beach chair, even leaning on Jim the entire way.

I stopped at the foot of the monstrosity and stared up at it.

"We could go get a seat on a bench," Jim suggested.

I shook my head. "Not a good enough view for sunset photos. People would be in my way."

I stared up at the chair a bit longer, trying to psych myself up for the climb up the three large rungs that made up the front of the chair below the seat.

"Those ones down there have the first rung at sand level," Jim pointed out.

"Tempting," I admitted. "But I would have to hobble through all that sand to get there." I looked him over appraisingly. "And I think the days of piggy backs are over."

"Way over," he answered, already ducking clear of the swat he saw coming.

As I scowled again at the increasingly offensive tourist attraction that called itself a chair, Jim went around me and put the camera bag up on the huge seat.

"How about I go first and help you from up there?"

I nodded and he nimbly climbed up and turned around, looking down at me expectantly. I sighed and placed my left foot on the first rung. I grabbed the second rung with both hands and heaved, wincing as I placed my right foot on the waiting support. I had repeated the process onto the second rung when Jim heaved me up to the seat on my belly, my feet sticking off the chair and flailing in the air like a floundering fish.

"As graceful as a ballerina," he teased.

"You landed yourself a big one," a gravelly voice called out. I rolled over clumsily and saw one of the ROMEO club members smiling up at us. It was the same man I'd stumbled into that first night we were here.

"No comment," Jim said diplomatically. "How are you Norm?" He hopped down into the sand to talk to the old-timer.

"Show off," I muttered. I took the opportunity to wiggle into a sitting position while the two men chatted, finally settling in against the large slatted chair back with an exhausted sigh. As I dug the camera out of its bag, I finally tuned in to what the men were saying.

"I wouldn't take too much stock into what gossip you overhear at a bar," Norm was saying to Jim.

"Not like the gossip you hear over coffee," Jim quipped.

Norm laughed good-naturedly, not minding the little dig at the ROMEO club. "Exactly!" He looked out over the lake. He held up his hand and measured the distance between the sun and the water with his fingers. "Not much time left before sunset," he observed. "I'd better be going if I want to avoid that screeching they call music."

My ears perked up. "Not a fan?" I asked.

"Pfft," Norm showed his disdain clearly. "I'll just go south down the beach. I won't be able to hear it past the gazebo if I turn the hearing aid off." His eyes twinkled. "It is one of the few times I appreciate the cursed thing." He gazed out over the lake. "And I do enjoy a nice, QUIET sunset."

He waved and moved on down the beach. He was much more spry than I was at the moment, I noticed.

"Gosh, he doesn't sound like a suspect at all," I muttered sarcastically.

"Let's just forget about it for tonight," Jim pleaded as he all but leapt up into the chair beside me.

"Where is the fun in that?" Marie's voice came from below. She had the most interesting timing, I thought to myself. I leaned over the railing and smiled down at her, both of us ignoring Jim's put-upon sigh.

"Come on up!" I invited, and soon she took the last spot on the chair, trapping Jim between the two of us.

"I'm not sure we thought this seating plan through," Jim complained, clearly anticipating being caught in the middle of non-stop chatter.

I kissed his cheek. "Worry not, wretched one, I'll be taking pictures."

I scooted forward on my behind, careful not to bend my knee, and perched on the end of the chair. My left foot rested on the top rung of the chair's ladder and my right leg stuck out in the air. Marie joined me at the edge with her camera.

"Don't you have enough sunset pics?" I asked.

"Don't you?" she countered. She smiled and turned to face the other direction, lowering her feet down to stand on the top rung, her thighs resting against the seat of the chair. "I'm going to get some shots of the piper," she explained.

"Show off," I said for the second time, envying her mobility and wishing my knee didn't hurt so much.

The sun was a reddish-orange ball and it was nearing the water on the horizon. Behind us, the first strains of the bagpipes filled the air and a few people cheered. Both of our cameras began clicking with the beat as we took photos in our respective directions. I heard the motor of Marie's camera as she zoomed in for a closer shot. Jim sighed and I heard his back hit the chair as he relaxed.

It was quite a peaceful scene, overall. At least it was right up until the sound of gunshots rent the air.

I jumped in shock and as a result lurched forward, losing my balance. My finger didn't stop holding down the button on the camera as I plummeted down and landed with a grunt in the sand.

The Travelling Klutz

With its glorious sunsets, crystal clear waters, pristine parks and unique downtown shops, cafes, and patios, the small town of Kincardine is the ideal place to get some R&R.

That would be rest and relaxation, of course. Or it could stand for rest and recuperation, if you are prone to injury like some people. Either way, there is no better spot for R&R than Kincardine's shoreline community.

You can rest on the sand at Station Beach, or on a giant chair at either of the two beaches flanking the piers. On a calm day you can get yourself an air mattress and float on the water. You can sit in any of the number of parks scattered through town. Or you can find a spot on a patio or at a coffee shop and sip your favourite beverage.

And if you happen to learn something interesting while you are getting your R & R, well, that is just what we call serendipity.

Chapter 9

Somehow, the old instinct of 'protect the camera at all costs' that journalists develop over their careers, kicked in for me. Combine that with the newfound need to protect my right knee and I somehow managed to roll slightly to my left as I hit the beach sand.

My hip and shoulder took the brunt of this most recent fall, the back of the camera cradled protectively against my chest and taking photos the entire way down thanks to the death grip I had on the shutter-release button. Of course, my hip and behind were already bruised from the two earlier falls, causing me to yelp in both shock and pain, even though the thick, fine sand did cushion the fall somewhat, making it less jarring than it could have been. It could be that my yelp was as much from surprise as from pain.

Jim leapt from the top of the chair, once again showing off his superior mobility, to land easily in the sand behind me. Had I tried that, even in top form, I would have likely broken my neck, or at least sprained an ankle. We both ignored the building cries of alarm from others on the beach as he once again checked me for broken bones.

"Are you okay?"

I groaned. "I think so."

He was helping me sit up when Marie scrambled down the chair's rungs to stand next to us.

"I've got to go," she announced, before looking at me in concern. "You okay?

I nodded in understanding and in answer, both. "You go. I have my knight in sandy armour here." I smiled up at Jim, who shook his head at me in exasperation.

Marie smiled briefly. "Good thing." She turned towards the parking lot. "Keep your cell phone on," she said, knowing how I was apt to forget to turn it on for days. "I'll keep you posted."

And then she was gone. My head was spinning, and not just from the most recent fall.

"Did someone else get shot?" I asked Jim.

"Looks that way," he answered. "Another Phantom Piper. Can you get up?"

I shook my head. "I think I'll stay here for a bit," I moaned. I looked over at the lighthouse, wincing as I turned my neck. "Do you think Marie got pictures of it happening? She was pointing her camera in that direction."

Jim shrugged. "Don't know. Don't really care right now. I'm more worried about you." He sat behind me, his back resting against a leg of the chair, and I turned to face the water, leaning back into him with a sigh. We sat in silence for a minute as I took stock of my limbs.

"I'll be ok," I assured him at the end of my inventory, wiggling my toes just to check.

I felt, more than heard, him sigh. "You will not let it go for a minute, will you?"

I shook my head and waited for him to answer my question. Finally he added, "No. I have no idea. Knowing her, she probably got a close up shot of it happening."

I wiggled my toes into the sand, more relieved than I would like to admit that I was able to do so. Not that I would tell Mr. Worrywart that.

"You know what this means?"

Jim squeezed his arms around me in a gentle hug. "That a piper got shot or that you can move your toes?"

I should have known he wouldn't have missed my toe wiggles. "The piper."

"What does it mean?"

I turned stiffly and looked up at him. "It means," I explained, "the last shooting likely wasn't personal. And it means that there's a serial piper sniper out there."

We sat in the coffee shop the next afternoon, my hands wrapped around a steaming cup of hot chocolate topped with two inches of whipped cream and chocolate shavings. The friendly young woman at the counter had been surprised to get the order, as it was currently 31°C outside, but was able to come up with my comfort drink quickly. She even added the chocolate shavings without my having to ask. I made sure to leave her a big tip.

My eyes were fixed on the vanilla cupcake in front of me, with its one inch topping of butter icing and brightly coloured sprinkles. I had already devoured the donut they had included with the hot drink and was feeling less sorry for myself as a result, if not less sore. Jim wisely kept any comments to himself about my less than healthy comfort eating as he sat across from me nursing his boring coffee.

"Do you and your cupcake need privacy?"

I looked up to see Marie approaching our table, her own equally boring coffee and donut in hand. I didn't bother to dignify that with an answer, since she was quite familiar with my relationship with both hot chocolate and cupcakes.

"So?" I asked as I peeled the wrapper from the bottom of the cupcake.

Marie raised her eyebrows. "I texted you."

"Hmph," I said around a mouthful of cupcake.

"I told you to make sure your phone was on."

I shrugged. "I was kind of busy ..."

"... feeling sorry for herself," Jim finished the sentence for me. I kicked him lightly under the table, wincing slightly at the resulting twinge of pain in my knee.

Marie sighed in frustration. "Whatever," she muttered. Then she leaned in conspiratorially and whispered. "The piper is alive!"

I stuffed half of the bottom of the cupcake into my mouth and motioned for her to continue.

"She - it was a woman this time - was shot in the shoulder," Marie said. "Oddly, the shooter didn't seem to be as sharp this time."

"I see what you did there," I acknowledged. "Sharp shooter."

"It's good someone gets my puns. Anyway, by the time I got there, the paramedics were putting her in the ambulance."

"It must have been a chore to get her down that spiral staircase," I observed. "Or did they drop her over the railing to a bunch of firemen waiting with a net?" Laughing at my own joke, I sprayed crumbs over the table. "Sorry," I mumbled.

Marie smirked at me. "No, nothing like that. I assume she was able to walk down herself, but that is something to check into." She pulled out her reporter's spiral notebook and jotted something down.

"Who is she?" Jim asked after seeing that my mouth was full again and picking up the slack.

Marie flipped through her notebook to check, but before she could say anything we were surrounded by the ROMEOs. The four of them pulled up chairs around the long table without being invited and settled in.

"Stacey McAllister," Norm supplied the answer. "She's been in the band for a year or so. One of the new crop of musicians they've been training."

Marie didn't seem to mind being upstaged. "Other than the pipe band, did she have any connection to the first victim?"

I slurped whipped cream off my hot chocolate and sat back, happy to just listen.

"No, not that we know of," Larry, the tall and thin ROMEO, answered. "She works at the plant, and arrived in town after he went off to school, so they didn't seem to run in the same circles."

A younger man approached the table. He stood at about six feet, and was strikingly handsome with short dark hair and a ready smile that brought out his dimples. He accepted the chair Larry pulled out for him. "Thanks Larry," he said. "How are you now?"

"Can't complain, Luke," Larry answered. "No one would listen anyhow."

That drew good natured chuckles from the men. I got the distinct impression this was some type of traditional greeting.

Luke nodded at the man I thought looked like Shatner. "Andrew."

He nodded back. "Luke."

Luke then turned his nod to the Santa look-alike. "Chris."

Seriously? I thought.

Chris 'Kringle' nodded back. "Luke." Okay, I didn't know his last name, but if the beard fits...

Now that the greetings were over, Marie turned to the newcomer. "You're in the pipe band, right?"

He nodded and quickly swallowed the bite of donut he had just taken. "Drummer," he said.

"Well, you should be safe," Norm mumbled.

Luke blanched. "I hope so," he said. "I don't mind telling you, this has all of us freaked out."

We all nodded at him in sympathy. "Will the band be marching on Saturday night?" I asked, concerned. We were only here for a week and I needed photos of the parade. Of course I was worried for the band members too. I'm not a monster.

"There's a meeting tomorrow between the band and the police to discuss it," Luke answered.

I nodded. "We're only here for a week, and I need to get photos of the parade for my article," I explained.

"Hopefully the shooter will be in custody by then," Marie said. "So, do you know if Matt and Stacey were connected at all?" She turned the conversation back to the victims.

Luke shook his head. "Besides being in the band, I'm pretty sure they don't hang out together whenever Mattl is home." He frowned. "Or they didn't, I guess."

"Wait, what did you call him?" I interrupted. "Mattel? He goes by a toy company's name?"

Luke chuckled. "Not Mattel ... Mattl. Pronounced like tattle. There were so many Matts in high school when we were there, that we added his last initial to his name to know who we were talking about," he explained. "And it just stuck with him."

"We overheard some gossip about ... Mattl," Jim looked at Luke for confirmation and he nodded. "... having an affair with a married woman." I nodded my support, and then winced from the effort.

"Well, Stacey isn't married," Norm stated, "so if that rumour is true, which I doubt, she wasn't the woman involved."

"There's the fact that they both piped down the sun," Jim stated the obvious.

We pondered that for a moment. My cupcake was gone and I sipped my hot chocolate before asking, "Do all of the pipers take a turn?"

Luke sipped his coffee, and then shook his head. "Not everyone wants to do it, and those who do have to be at a certain level of ability before they get the gig," he explained. "There's a sign up list that circulates around and you choose the days you want to do it before the summer season starts. But being up there solo can be nerve wracking, so they really encourage only experienced pipers to play the lighthouse." He paused to take another sip of his coffee. "Usually you need to have marched in a year of parades first. It really depends on how much you practice and how confident you are."

We all nodded sagely. That seemed logical.

"What about being able to play loud enough?" I asked.

Luke shook his head. "Volume is pretty much the same on all pipes. But they do have an experienced piper at the bottom to tune you up before you make the climb. It can take years before you get an ear for that."

"Didn't you say that Stacey is fairly new?" Marie asked, writing frantically in her notebook as she spoke.

"Yes, but she's a natural," Luke answered. "She reached the level of a lot more experienced pipers pretty quickly, so they waived the year of marching with the band thing for her."

"But not everyone is," I said, and then clarified when I got quizzical looks. "A natural."

"We all develop at our own rate," Luke shrugged.

Jim and Marie stared at me.

"I know that look," Marie said.

"What are you thinking?" Jim added.

"If there's no connection between the two victims, it can't be personal," I began.

"We said that already," Marie pointed out dryly.

"And if it's just that the victims are pipers..."

"Then someone hates pipers!" Marie concluded.

"Assuming there's only one shooter," Jim added, throwing a wrench into our speculation.

"Don't look now," Norm said, his voice full of warning.

I looked anyway. Then I cursed. "I SO don't need this right now."

"Are you two spreading rumours?" Detective Wolsey's voice would have frozen my hot chocolate, had there been any left.

"Three," Jim said.

"What?"

"Three," he repeated. "You keep forgetting to include me." Jim looked at me. "Should I be insulted?"

Marie and I both stifled a chuckle.

Wolsey didn't find it funny. "Are you THREE spreading rumours?" he growled.

"Would we do that De-tec-tive?" Marie asked sweetly.

When I didn't chime in, Wolsey glared in my direction. "What? No witty follow-up? What's wrong with you?"

"I fell."

He gave me an eye roll that a teenage girl would be proud to perform. "That's nothing new."

I noticed out of the corner of my eye that the ROMEOs and Luke were clearing out of the line of fire as we spoke. The cowards.

"Three times in as many days is a new record for Casey," Jim supplied fondly, reaching over and rubbing my back.

"Impressive," Wolsey retorted, turning back to Marie. "Stay out of our way," he warned, turning to leave.

"De-tec-tive," I piped up. It seemed I wasn't too sore to jump in after all. "Can you tell us how Stacey is doing?"

He turned back, a frown firmly in place. "How do you know..."

Marie simply nodded in the direction of the ROMEOs, who were on their way out the door. "It's a small town," she said.

"I'll put out a press release when we're ready," Wolsey growled at her, turning again to leave.

Not so fast, I thought. I looked quickly at Marie, and then we hit him with simultaneous questions.

"Is Stacey going to be okay?"

"Is her condition stable?"

"Is she in intensive care?"

"Is she allowed visitors?"

Wolsey turned and stared at us for a moment. "It doesn't matter how many different ways you ask the same question," he snarled, "you will still get the same answer." He turned again to leave, frustration clearly beginning to show in his posture.

But we weren't done with him yet.

"Do the victims have anything to connect them?"

"Do you know where the shot came from?"

"Were the shots from the same gun?"

Wolsey whipped around, exasperated, his face red. "NO!" he snapped. "How could it be the same gun when you supposedly tripped over the first one?"

We all stared at him in shock, Marie and I both uncharacteristically speechless. Realizing what he had just let out of the bag, Wolsey turned even redder, with what I assumed to be fury combined with embarrassment.

"Stay. Out. Of. It." he ordered in staccato. Then he stormed out of the coffee shop.

Marie grinned in glee, writing in her notebook as fast as her hand could move.

"Well, THAT couldn't have gone any better!"

The Travelling Klutz

Kincardine residents have always liked their slogans, and so have visitors to the town, because those slogans ring true for most of the people who hear them.

The slogan 'Where You're a Stranger Only Once' spoke to the friendly, welcoming nature of the residents. This is a town where people smile and nod to you when you pass by, where there is always someone willing to lend a hand, where the greeting 'How are you now?' is one that is almost universal.

In 2012, the pipe band came up with a witty slogan, 'Trust us, it's big', to promote the Saturday night pipe band parades. It was accompanied in advertising by the photo of a kilt wearing man, from the waist down and could be found on everything from giant billboards to postcards. The double entendre, of course, was not lost on anyone, hinting at a sense of humour, and a naughty one at that.

In 2016 the municipality took inspiration from the pipe band's branding success and released a campaign that declared the Scottish area 'Pants Optional'. Various depictions of the slogan appeared alongside photos of people of various ages, doing any number of activities available in the town, wearing a tartan kilt.

And in case you are wondering, Kincardine does not have a nude beach in its boundaries.

The Celtic words 'Cead Mille Failte' greet visitors to Victoria Park from atop the western entrance pergola. Meaning 'A hundred thousand welcomes', they represent both the Scottish heritage of the town and the friendliness of its residents. The pergola is a favourite spot for photographers, with a number of wedding parties posing there throughout the spring, summer and fall.

Another slogan you will hear about town, but mostly down at the marina, is 'Where You Can Eat What You Catch'. This catch phrase is a testament to the crystal clear waters of 'Ontario's West Coast', a regional moniker referring to the Canadian shoreline of Lake Huron. When the water is calm, you can wade out up to your waist and still see your feet as clearly as if you were standing in your bathtub. In fact, you can clearly see the wreck of the schooner Ann Maria at Station Beach. The ship sank south of the town's piers in 1902 and her skeleton remains for all to see to this day. For anglers, such clean water bodes well for the health of the fish stock in the lake.

When you are out in a boat, on a paddle board, or just going for a swim, you will be able to see all sorts of things under the water. Keep an eye out for everything from interesting rocks to various types of fish, and in rare cases even more shocking surprises.

Chapter 10

We went to the cottage to rest after a long and eventful day. Not to mention painful as well, for me at least. Although a bath was tempting, this time I opted for a shower to ease away my aches; a soak in a tub would have taken too much time. While I was enjoying the heat of the water, Jim ordered takeout from the popular Erie Belle: a British style fish and chip restaurant downtown.

The restaurant is named for the wreck of the Erie Belle, a Great Lakes steam ship that exploded and sank off shore in 1883. At that time, a number of powerful storms wracked the area. The Belle, as it is affectionately referred to locally, was attempting to aid a schooner that had run ashore south of town. Reports are contradictory as to the cause, but the Belle's boiler exploded, killing four and throwing eight overboard to be rescued by the very ship they were trying to help. The boiler from the ship remains in the water at the aptly named Boiler Beach, and is a frequently photographed spot for visitors.

I got out of the shower and dressed, to find that Jim had gone to pick up our order. I brought out my laptop and transferred the day's photos to its hard drive, then started looking through them on the larger screen to see if I had anything good for my article. The big beach chair did indeed prove to be an excellent vantage point for the sunset photos, and I realized that I was going to be hard pressed to choose only a couple to send to my editor. One in particular, taken before I had scooted forward on the chair, caught Jim's and my feet in front of the tan sand and blue water that was as still as glass. The sun was just starting to set in the photo, and the reds and oranges were still pale as they splashed across distant wispy clouds, giving the photo the aura of an ageless oil painting.

I flipped through the pictures until I came to the spot where I had fallen off the chair. I winced at the memory. Even sitting alone in the cottage, my cheeks burned with embarrassment. I just could not believe that I could fall down when I was just sitting still. With a sigh, I looked at the photos I had taken during my tumble from (disputable) grace.

One seemed to be a close up of sand, but it was blurry so I wasn't entirely sure. I deleted it, with satisfaction. The next photo was a surprisingly clear shot of the lake, showing a small boat between our position and the pier, just out a bit from the wreck of the schooner Ann Maria. It was a sideways shot, and I turned my head to get a better look.

The next photo was a shot of the sky and a bit of the blue chair, likely taken just before I hit the ground. The final picture had captured the shirt I had been wearing, its 'Life is Good' logo partly visible, no doubt the result of my attempt to save the camera by cradling it to my body. I shook my head and chuckled at myself.

"What's so funny?" Jim asked, entering the cottage accompanied by the mouth watering smell of fish and chips.

"The pictures of my fall," I answered, getting up and going to the refrigerator. "Beer?"

"Please," Jim answered. "Want to eat outside?"

I nodded and followed him out, grabbing some plates and utensils on my way. I cradled the craft beer against my body, and then put all of it down on the picnic table. I cracked my own beer open as he unwrapped our dinner and set it out for us.

I'd ordered the haddock and chips, with a side of gravy, my favourite from the restaurant's menu. I quickly placed the food on my plate and, cutting off the end of a piece of haddock, I popped it into my mouth with a happy moan at its hot, crispy goodness.

"Hungry?" Jim teased as he placed his food on his plate in a more orderly fashion.

I nodded as I dumped the gravy onto the fries and stabbed some with my fork. "I need food," I rationalized. "I'm healing."

He opened a ketchup packet and squeezed some onto his fries. "You seem to be moving a bit better," he observed, digging into his battered cod.

"The shower helped," I slurred past a mouthful of gravy soaked fries.

"Not to mention the beer," he added. I held mine up to him for a toast.

"To beer," we said together.

"The cause of, and solution to, all of life's problems," Jim added with a grin.

Before I could think of a witty retort, Mrs. Holmberg popped out from behind a bush. Had she been spying on us?

"I thought I smelled food from The Belle!" she said by way of a greeting.

"Hello, Mrs. Holmberg, how are you tonight?" Jim asked politely while I stuffed my mouth with food to ensure that I wouldn't say anything rude.

"Oh well, fine, thank you. Although I'm craving fish and chips now." She looked longingly at our food. She snapped out of her reverie suddenly and announced, "I think I'll make my way down to the Belle! Thanks for the idea!"

And she was gone as quickly as she had appeared. I laughed. "She must be a retired ninja," I told Jim.

"She does come and go quickly," he agreed.

After a few minutes of silent eating, he asked, "Anything interesting in your pictures?"

"I got quite a few nice sunset shots."

"Not what I meant."

I smiled at him. "I know." I thought back through the pictures I had looked at. "There was one sideways one I took as I fell," I said, frowning. "There was something ... it was of a boat, out past the wreck ... and I keep thinking I missed something when I looked at it."

Jim gathered up the garbage from our takeout packaging in one hand and his meal in the other. "Well, let's go check it out."

I took my plate and beer back into the dining room and settled in at the computer, taking the last swig of beer. Jim went to get us each another and I brought up the picture in question. He came to stand behind me and looked over my shoulder.

"Turn it ninety degrees."

With a few clicks of the mouse I turned the photo's orientation and we both stared at it, stunned silent for a moment.

"Well, I'll be darned," he muttered.

I looked at the flash of light I'd caught emanating from the deck of the boat floating parallel to the beach and the lighthouse.

"I'm so glad you see it too," I whispered.

While I called Marie, Jim went to have a shower. Marie was knocking on our door so soon after I called her that I wondered if she had been camping out in the back yard.

"I was on my way when you called," she explained upon seeing my surprised look.

I waved her into the room. "Why? What's up?"

"My pictures," she said. "I got a close up of the piper being shot!"

"No way!"

"Way!"

She plopped down at the kitchen table, pushed my laptop to the side and replaced it with her own. As she opened it up, she asked," "What's up with you? You sounded kind of cryptic when you called."

Her photo popped up on the monitor of her computer and I leaned in for a closer look.

"Surely, you're not going to use that," I said as I looked at the photo. "It's way too graphic."

"I know," she agreed regretfully. "And stop calling me Shirley."

"Not to mention that it would make Wolsey's head explode," I added with a smirk.

Marie looked thoughtful. "There is that."

"No." I shook my head emphatically.

She sighed. "I know. But just think of his reaction."

"You'd likely get arrested. He'd find some way to pin the shootings on you."

She chuckled in agreement.

"And me as an accessory," I added.

"Who is an accessory?" Jim asked, coming in from the rear of the cottage. His hair was still damp and he looked so handsome I stopped to admire the view. "And accessory to what exactly? Because with the two of you involved, it has to be something."

Marie pointed to her computer screen and he leaned over her shoulder to look at the photo on the screen. After a second he gave a low whistle. "You're not using that, right?"

"No," Marie answered. "But it is an amazing shot."

"Don't sound so disappointed," Jim admonished. "I'm sure you have other shots."

Marie flipped through the other photos until she came to one of the piper leaning against the railing, the pipes visible through the railing on the floor, and an ambulance and police car on the road directly below. "I thought I'd use this one," she said, sounding a little disappointed.

"That looks good," Jim concurred. "Plus, you still have Casey's photo."

Marie snapped out of her funk. "What photo?"

"You'd have seen it if you hadn't pushed my lap top out of the way when you came in," I teased her. I shoved her laptop aside, experiencing a bit of satisfaction as I did so, and moved mine back in front of her. I opened it up and showed her the sideways version of the photo.

She tilted her head to the side and stared. "Is that a boat?"

"Yep," Jim and I both said. I reached over and brought up the next, right-side-up photo for her to study.

"Is that what I think it is?" she asked incredulously.

We both nodded, grinning.

"How do you keep catching these moments?"

I shrugged. "What happened to this town that I keep catching these terrible moments with my camera?" I countered.

"That sounds like a subject for my next editorial," Marie mumbled. "You'll have to buy the paper to read my answer." She turned back to the photo. "Did you call the De-tec-tive?"

I suppressed an involuntary shudder. "No, I called the press." I hesitated, and then added, "Do you think this would make that red-faced head of his explode?"

Marie laughed and Jim rolled his eyes. "It might cause a minor heart attack, tops. Is it premeditated murder if we do something to cause his death but don't expect him to die?"

Jim jumped in. "We have to tell him."

I sighed. "Do you think I can just send him an e-mail?" I pulled my laptop from in front of Marie and gave her a mischievous look. "This way, I can cc the press."

Marie laughed. Jim winced.

"Well, I have a paper that goes out in the morning, a new front page photo to use, AND a new editorial to write." Marie headed for the door. "What are you two up to tomorrow?"

Jim nodded in my direction. "Casey wants to swim from the pier to the beach," he said.

"That is if my injured body is up to it," I clarified.

"A night's rest and you will be fine," Marie assured me. "I wish I could join you, but I have lots of work to do. Enjoy!"

Marie was right, I realized the next morning as we headed to the beach. I was stiff, and my knee still ached quite a bit, but I was feeling much better than I had the night before. I was sure that once I got into a swimming rhythm, the sore, tight muscles would loosen up.

It was about 11 a.m. when we parked at Station Beach and crossed over the boardwalk and into the sand of the beach. The plan was to leave our towels on the beach just south of the ship wreck and walk onto the nearest pier. From there we would jump in and swim to our spot on the beach on a diagonal line, passing close enough to the wreck to get a good look on our way by.

It was a beautiful day for a swim and a number of people were in the water and on the piers. The water was once again like glass, with barely a breeze in the air to cause much more than a tiny ripple. Had it been wavy we would have postponed our swim, due in part to poor visibility but mostly to the possibility of rip tides at the beach when the water is rough. That was definitely not a worry on this day, however.

We spread out our large beach towels on the sand, taking off our shoes and using them to weigh down the towels so they wouldn't blow away, adding a few rocks for good measure. I took my goggles from their case and replaced them with my glasses, putting the case in my shoe for safe keeping. Without my glasses the scene around me took on a slightly hazy appearance, but I couldn't wear them and swim efficiently. Instead I had my Speedo Optical goggles, which allowed me to see clearly in the water.

We headed down to the water, keeping off the sand that was already surprisingly hot on bare feet, and walked towards the pier. We passed children splashing in the water under the watchful eyes of parents, and people setting up for a picnic lunch under the watchful eyes of a number of sea gulls. The concrete pier was hot on the feet and we walked to the end of the structure as quickly as my aches and pains allowed. On the way we passed a few dedicated anglers casting their lines off the side, and a few kids tossing stones into the water. Soon we were at the end of the pier, looking down into the deep blue water lapping gently at its side.

"Let's count to three," Jim suggested. "One..."

"Wait!"

"What?"

"Are we jumping on three or after we've counted to three?"

He looked at me in annoyance. "Again, what?"

"Is it one, two, jump? Or one, two, three, jump?"

Jim sighed. "Only you," he muttered. "ON three."

"So one, two, jump." I did my best to conceal my amusement at his frustration.

"Keep it up and I'm pushing you in," he growled.

I laughed and we counted together.

"One, two ..." We jumped as we yelled 'three' in mid air.

The water was a bit of a shock, being one of the Great Lakes and always a tad bit on the chilly side, but we quickly acclimated. I pulled on my goggles while treading water and Jim followed suit with his snorkelling mask.

"Ready?" I asked.

"On three?" he countered.

I laughed and set out, leaving him in my wake, albeit briefly. He quickly caught up and we swam side by side.

At first we saw a few boulders around the base of the pier, no doubt placed there to prevent erosion of the structure. Soon the bottom was rippled sand, sculpted into patterns by the movement of the water. Every now and then one of us would point out a fish or, sadly, some debris discarded on the lake bottom.

We continued on, the water muffling the sounds from the beach, the boats, and the paddle boards splashing about, so that it was easy to imagine that we were the last two people on the earth. For a bit we held hands and flutter kicked along like snorkelers, and a contentment came over us at this shared experience. But Jim had a stronger kick than I did, given the sore knee, so we let go of each other with an affectionate squeeze and continued on at our own pace.

I was so lulled into the 'zone' that I often hit when swimming that I swam right into Jim where he'd stopped and was treading water, waiting for me.

"Hey!" I said.

"Hey yourself!" he answered, pulling me into his arms. I hugged him back and we bobbed down into the water as a result. We resurfaced, laughing and sputtering. I drifted away from him, but he reached over and pulled me back. When his lips met mine I marvelled at how he could still make my heart race, and I told him so.

He chuckled, obviously pleased. "It is either the kiss or the exercise," he teased.

"Definitely the kiss," I said, kissing him softly before letting go and taking stock of our progress. "We're about half way."

"Two thirds if we go directly in from here," he pointed out. "How are your muscles and knee?"

"Good," I assured him. "The swim has loosened things up. We can keep going to where the towels are." I rolled over and floated on my back. "This is the life," I sighed.

He reached over and nudged me. "Let's get going."

I rolled back over and splashed him. "Getting tired old man?"

He splashed back. "Never," he answered, and then he was off, leaving me in his wake this time.

I started to race after him, but a glint on the lake bottom caught the corner of my eye. I slowed and turned away from the beach to check it out. As I got closer to the spot, I was sure that what I was seeing on the bottom was a long piece of metal. I stopped and treaded water, glancing back to see where I was in relation to Jim.

I was a little west of the ship wreck. Jim was about 20 metres away along our original diagonal path to shore. As I watched, I saw him stop and search for me.

"Over here," I yelled, waving to him.

I saw him shake his head and turn to swim back to my position. When he reached me, he sounded perturbed. "What are you doing?"

"I, uh, found something."

"It had better be treasure."

"Not exactly."

He frowned and looked down into the water below my feet. After a moment he put his face in the water for a better look. He resurfaced, took off the mask and stared at me in shock.

"There is never a dull moment with you, my sweet."

"I wasn't looking for it," I protested.

"And yet here it is and you found it. Well, let's go to shore and report it."

I shook my head. What I was about to say was not going to go over well.

"If we both go, we might not find it again."

He frowned. "I don't swim a kilometre or two at a time, three times a week, like some people. I can't stay out here much longer."

"Then don't," I said. "I'm nowhere near my limit, and you know that I couldn't sink even if I tried." My heart warmed at the clear worry on his face at the thought of splitting up. "I'll be fine. You swim straight to shore, and remember to roll onto your back and scull if you get tired. Go to the car and get a cell phone. I'll be right here over top of this spot when you bring the cavalry."

"The cavalry? In water?"

"Maybe they'll be riding seahorses," I joked.

He sighed. "More like the police boat."

I reached out and pushed him, causing us to drift away from each other. "The sooner you go, the sooner I can come in." I looked under the water and then swam back to where I was directly over the object.

"Okay," Jim said as he turned. "You should use the time alone to figure out how to explain this to Wolsey." He glanced back and wryly added, "He is NOT going to be thrilled that you're the one who has found another rifle."

The Travelling Klutz

A wonderful aspect of living or vacationing in a lakeside town is the opportunity it affords to get out on the water.

In Kincardine, the crystal clear waters beckon to boaters of varied types. There are fishing boats that venture out early in the morning in search of that prized salmon or trout. That group of people, the anglers, effectively take over the town during the two large fishing derbies: one held in the spring and the other in summer.

A stroll along the floating docks of the marina will show you just how many pleasure boats ply the waters of Lake Huron from the Kincardine harbour. You will see everything from sailboats to speedboats, catamarans to cabin cruisers, hydrofoils to houseboats, and jet boats to yachts. Occasionally, you will find visiting schooners that sail from port to port on the Great Lakes. Also launching from the harbour area are canoes and kayaks, sail and paddle boards, kite and surf boards, paddle and inflatable boats, rafts, and zodiacs. You name it, if it floats, you will likely find it off the Kincardine shore.

While those boats are recreational, there are also those that serve the public. Sailing from the harbour are commercial fishing boats and charter fishing tour boats. There is a rescue boat operating out of this marina, which is pressed into service along with numerous smaller vessels, to patrol the water during events such as the Women's Triathlon or the Reunion Swim to the Breakwall. It is always a good sign to see the rescue boat tied to the dock, as that means no one is in trouble on the vast waters of the Great Lake.

And of course, there is a police marine unit that patrols the waters and answers calls of all sorts. They can respond to accidents, stranded boats, drinking and boating offences, and more.

Because you just never know what you will find above or below the waves.

Chapter 11

I spent the time alone in the water, as Jim had suggested, anticipating the scene that would no doubt occur when Wolsey found out what I had come across this time. I worried that he would decide I would be less of a bother to him sitting in a jail cell for a night or two. My muscles started to ache again just thinking of the cots in a jail cell.

I watched Jim swim directly to shore, shrinking in size as he got further away from me. I wasn't worried about being alone in the lake myself; the water was calm and the weather was clear. I did worry about him, however. He only swam when we were on vacation, a total of a handful of times a year. So I was more relieved than I would ever admit to him when I saw him walk up onto the beach. He turned and waved, a small, blurry figure on the beach, and I waved back, knowing that without my glasses, he could see me better than I could see him. I put my goggles back on and looked again, just to be sure I was looking at the right person.

It wasn't long afterwards that I saw the police boat heading my way. The police must have been at the marina already. As they got close my heart sank. Right there at the front of the boat was the perpetually scowling Detective Wolsey. He reminded me a bit of the Incredible Hulk. He had taken his suit jacket off in the heat and tossed it carelessly onto a nearby bench. You could clearly see his ample belly protruding over his waistband and revolver resting in its holster on his hip. His shirt was as wrinkled as his jacket and was becoming stained with perspiration. He was accompanied by a man wearing the summer police uniform of a blue short sleeved shirt and dark shorts, looking dashingly handsome. While he piloted the boat, another man was at the rear of the boat with his back to me, donning SCUBA gear. I assumed the first man was the captain of the vessel, while the other was clearly the diver. As they got closer, I removed the goggles from my eyes and rested them on my forehead.

"So where is this find of yours?" Wolsey demanded the second the boat captain dropped anchor.

"I am fine De-tec-tive, thank you for your concern," I retorted. "I can tread water a little longer."

He ignored me and silently waited for an answer to his question.

I frowned back at him. "It's right under my feet," I told him, then donned my goggles and stuck my face in the water to be sure. I popped back up and said, "Yep. Still there. I stayed here, alone I might add, to make sure it would be easy for your diver to find."

"I appreciate that ma'am," the other man on the boat spoke up. He had a SCUBA tank on his back and a mask propped up on his forehead, the diving regulator mouthpiece dangling over his shoulder. He made his way to the back of the boat to don his flippers. Before I knew it he had jumped into the water and reached my position. He submerged briefly for a look, resurfaced long enough to give the Detective a thumbs-up, and then disappeared beneath the water to retrieve the gun.

I swam over to the back of the boat. "Permission to come aboard?" I asked, hopefully keeping the sarcasm from my tone.

Wolsey waved a hand in my direction without bothering to spare me a glance, which I took to mean 'Come aboard' instead of 'Get lost'. I scrambled up onto the platform. When I stood up I realized how tired I actually was: my legs felt like spaghetti noodles. I walked onto the deck of the boat, stumbling a bit as I got my sea legs. Of course, I banged into Wolsey's back in the process. He was leaning out over the side of the boat watching the diver and didn't see me coming. He came close to pitching over the side and into the water, but saved himself at the last minute. You can't have it all, apparently.

"Bloody hell!" he exploded, before turning his full attention on me. "What is it with you?" he fairly roared, causing me to back away quickly into the bench on the opposite side of the boat. I fell onto the seat with an audible 'oof', splashing water all over his discarded jacket in the process. I figured I was doing him a favour. The water might take out the wrinkles.

I glared back at him. I was very quickly reaching my limit for aggravation. I saw the captain head to the front of the boat, as far away from us as he could get. Wise man.

"What is it with YOU?" I yelled back at him. "Do you even know how to act like a decent human being?"

I could almost see his blood pressure rising. He was clearly shocked at getting some of his own attitude thrown back at him. He moved across the boat towards me, stumbling slightly as he did so. I smirked at him. "Not as easy as it looks, is it?"

He shook his finger in my face. "You are obstructing a police investigation," he growled, ignoring my jibe. "I could throw you in jail."

I stood to face him, wobbling a bit in the process. He was the one to back away this time, and I took comfort in the fact that he seemed to be nervous around me. I shook my finger back at him for good measure.

"If it weren't for the photos I GAVE YOU, and the evidence I FOUND ...

"Supposedly stumbled over," he interrupted.

"... for YOU," I continued as though he had not spoken, "you wouldn't even HAVE an investigation!"

"I'm still not convinced you're not involved with all of this!"

"Don't be an idiot!" I had officially lost the last of my patience with him, and Jim wasn't around to rein my reactions in.

I'd never know what Wolsey's response would have been because the sound of a man clearing his throat drew our attention to the platform at the back of the boat. The diver had resurfaced and brought with him a high powered rifle. He held it out towards us.

"Here's your evidence," he said. "We can head back in. There's nothing else down there."

Wolsey shuffled as far away from me as possible. I swear I heard him mumble "I should make you swim back" as he went.

The Travelling Klutz

The town of Kincardine is more than clean beaches, crystal clear water, and friendly faces. Should you, by some mischance, be injured while partaking in the town's many activities, or while walking down the street, rest assured that the town is well equipped to meet your medical needs.

Thanks to the presence of a nuclear power plant half an hour's drive north of the town, Kincardine is home to an up-to-date medical facility that many other towns its size would envy. Perched high on a hill at the north end of town, the hospital stands at the ready to treat patients, young and old, visitor or resident. It is the designated medical facility to be used in the event of an emergency at what locals refer to simply as 'the plant'. As such, it can deal with all sorts of emergencies that could arise, big or small.

Emergencies like slips and falls, or gunshot wounds. They are versatile that way.

Chapter 12

It was a tense, but quick, boat ride back to the harbour. The captain turned the boat around and headed north, rounding the nearest pier and heading through the channel formed by the two piers that guide boats towards the marina. I stayed at the stern of the boat with the police diver, who was much more easy-going than Wolsey, hoping his proximity would protect me from any more run-ins with the detective. I also hoped that I would be able to disembark quickly when we reached land, thus negating the need for protection from the grouchy detective at all.

We passed a sailboat on its way out of the harbour, and the people on board gave us a friendly wave as they went by. I thought I saw one man push a cooler under a bench as we neared the boat, and I chuckled in amusement. The police had other things to worry about than what kind of beverages the sailors had on board, however, and continued on to the harbour. Anglers and children waved cheerfully from the concrete structures, unaware of the discovery we had made or of the tense mood on board.

Ignorance truly is bliss.

As we approached the slip in front of the marina office and gas pumps, I saw with relief that Jim was waiting there for me. Even better, to my shivering self, was the sight of him holding my towel, clothing, and shoes.

I barely contained my laugh when I saw who was beside him. Marie had her camera aimed our way and was taking photos of every move we made.

"Oh, for the love of Pete!" Wolsey cursed behind me when he saw her on the dock.

I turned, glanced at him, and plastered on my sweetest smile. "Who's Pete?" I asked sweetly. "De-tec-tive, I had no idea you'd come out of the closet."

The diver behind me chuckled, but stopped quickly when Wolsey sent a nasty glare his way. That glare then swung back to me.

"I am not gay," he clarified through clenched teeth.

"Not that there's anything wrong with that," I quoted Seinfeld glibly.

He blinked and was silent long enough that I almost felt sorry for him. Almost.

He pointed his finger at me. "This is how rumours get started," he said. He then opted to ignore my existence and started barking orders around the boat. Had I not been so cold, I would have made the effort to be insulted.

The second the boat bumped into the dock side stoppers, I was off the boat and rushing into the waiting arms of my handsome hubby. By the strength of his returning hug, I could tell he was relieved to have me back on land as well.

"My hero," I said, and I meant it sincerely. I went up onto my toes and planted a soft kiss on his lips. "Have I told you how lucky I am to have you?"

"Not enough," he answered as he wrapped my towel around me. I turned and leaned against him, watching the police begin to disembark. Wolsey came ashore with the rifle in a giant, clear evidence bag. I was surprised that those things came in such a large size. Marie didn't miss a moment, her camera clicking away rapidly.

I hoped his sour look would come across in the photos.

"Break it up you two," he sneered in our direction, "or I'll arrest you for public indecency."

"Finally, something we agree on," Marie muttered, looking all the while as if the very concept of agreeing with Wolsey was making her feel ill.

"Would we get a conjugal cell?" Jim quipped before bending down and nuzzling my neck. I giggled, surprised that he seemed to be poking the bear this time.

Wolsey scowled and started to push past us. "Do NOT leave town," he snapped in passing.

I just flipped him the bird. I'm fairly certain that Marie got a photo of that too.

Marie invited us to tag along on a visit to interview the sniper's latest victim at the hospital, and we arranged for her to pick us up on the way. We then headed back to the cottage so I could have a hot shower and change my clothes.

Mrs. Holmberg was at the end of the driveways as though waiting to greet us.

"You look like a drowned rat," she told me with a chuckle.

"I went for a really long swim," I told her. "I'm really quite chilled."

"I'm not surprised. I heard you had to wait around in the water for the police to arrive."

Jim looked at her in shock. "How on earth did you hear that?"

"I have my ways," she said, looking mysterious.

I was more certain than ever that she had been a ninja. Possibly a ninja spy.

"Well, you go warm up dear. You don't want to catch a cold."

I was about to tell her you can't get a cold from being in the cold, but she'd already left.

"I'm glad I don't have to keep up with her," I muttered, heading towards the cottage and the waiting shower. I stayed in the shower until the hot water ran out and I finally felt warm again.

"So, my sweet, you didn't look too happy when you got off the boat," Jim observed as I entered the living room. "What happened?"

"Wolsey was an ass."

"What else is new?" Jim made room for me on the sofa, but I plopped down on his lap instead, resting my head on his shoulder. He planted a kiss on the top of my head.

"He wasn't always that way," I admitted, before forging ahead with my tale. "I was tired when he got there."

Jim chuckled. "And?"

"And I may not have handled things with my usual ... pizzazz," I explained, splaying the fingers of both hands wide in the air when I said the word 'pizzazz'.

Jim frowned, cupped my chin in his hand and lifted my head so he could look me in the eye. "What did you do?" There was an element of trepidation in his voice.

"I might have lost my balance and banged into him on the boat..."

Jim looked at me and patiently waited.

"... and almost knocked him overboard."

His jaw dropped. "That must have gone over well."

"Pretty much," I agreed with a shrug. "Then I might have told him it wouldn't hurt him to act like a decent person..."

Jim's eyes bulged.

"... then I shook MY finger in HIS face ... and ..."

"There's more?" Jim squeaked.

I plowed forward, wanting to get it all out now that I had started. "... and told him that he would have no evidence at all if it weren't for me ..." I hesitated.

"Is that all?"

"Not enough for you?"

Jim raised an eyebrow worthy of Spock from Star Trek.

"There is one more little thing..." I held up my thumb and fore finger, spaced a tiny bit apart, and drew out the word 'little'.

He squeezed the bridge of his nose in frustration. "And that would be what exactly?"

I looked down. "I may have called him an idiot," I mumbled.

Jim barked out a laugh. "And he didn't arrest you?"

"I'm pretty sure that insulting the police is not a crime," I said testily. When Jim just looked at me, waiting for more, I admitted, "He threatened to."

Jim sighed and shook his head at me.

"Oh! And then I flipped him off, but you saw that."

Laughter erupted from the other side of the screen door. We looked in that direction to see Marie almost doubled over, she was laughing so hard.

"I'd pay real money to see footage of all that," she gasped.

I grinned at her, glad someone appreciated my efforts at frustrating our favourite De-tec-tive.

"Well, now that I've had a good laugh," Marie added, "shall we go?"

We piled into Marie's car: me up front with her and Jim in the back despite my offer to let him ride shotgun.

"How did your photos at the marina turn out?" I asked as I fastened my seat belt.

"I got a pretty good one of Wolsey carrying the gun off the boat," she answered. "The diver is in the background holding his SCUBA gear."

"Oh, please tell me Wolsey looks pissed off in it," I begged.

"You know it! Really, does he ever look any other way?"

"When you two are around?" Jim piped up from the back seat. "No, he does not."

"That's enough from the peanut gallery," Marie shot back at him and he held up his hands in mock surrender.

She turned back to me. "So what do you think? Front page above the fold?"

I laughed. "That sounds perfect to me. Did you get one of me flipping him off?"

"I already e-mailed it to you."

"Awe, that's so sweet. Thank you."

The peanut gallery in the back seat cleared his throat. "Uh, ladies?" Jim said. "I have a question."

"Shoot," Marie called back to him.

I winced. "Unfortunate choice of words, given recent events," I pointed out.

Jim didn't give us a chance to debate semantics. "What exactly do you two have against Wolsey anyway?"

Marie and I looked at each other.

"Um, well, we swore to never speak of that." I looked pointedly at Marie.

"Especially to you," Marie added. At my glare, she mouthed, "Sorry."

Jim was frowning. "What did you swear to keep from me?"

I sighed. "Well, when you put it that way..." I said in resignation. "Okay, but don't laugh."

"Don't laugh too hard anyway," Marie added.

I ignored her. "Do you remember that trip you took to Houston for work?"

"Yes?" He drew out the word.

"While you were gone..."

"We decided to have a girls' night," Marie pitched in.

"And we got a bit tipsy," I added.

"From the rum..."

"And the wine..."

"The beer probably didn't help," I admitted. "And Marie had some Caesars."

Jim chuckled. "I know you two can get a bit crazy already."

"So we decided to walk from the bar back to your place," Marie picked up the story, "like responsible adults."

"But it had been raining..."

"And there was construction on Queen Street ..."

"It was muddy," I clarified.

"And we were tipsy," Marie stressed.

"Ya, I got that part," Jim said. "How does Wolsey fit into this tale?"

"He was a constable back then," Marie told him.

"How exactly did he make detective anyway?" I asked Marie.

"I know, eh?"

"Ladies! Focus!' Jim snapped.

"Right! So the constable was watching for drunk drivers coming from the bar," I continued.

"And directing traffic away from the construction," Marie added.

"Apparently he was versatile that way," I added sarcastically. I swear I could feel Jim glaring at me in frustration from the back seat, but didn't turn around to check.

"Anyway, a couple of drunken pedestrians crossed his path."

"She means us. He came over to us, to give us a warning or something..."

"And it was muddy ...."

"And we were tipsy ..."

Jim cleared his throat pointedly. Marie turned into the long driveway heading up the hill to the hospital as I continued the tale.

"I slipped in the mud ..."

"Of course you did," Jim muttered.

"...and I think he was reaching out to keep me upright," I added, ignoring his snide remark with effort.

"Which never ends well," Marie jumped on the Pick-On-Casey bandwagon as she pulled up to the parking lot gate. She lowered her window and pressed the button to get a parking pass. The gate rose and she drove through to the parking lot.

"No, it never does," Jim agreed, sounding like someone resigned to his fate. I had to give him that one, since he is the one often rescuing me from spills.

That doesn't mean I had to be happy about it. "Do you want to hear this or not?" I grumbled, shooting a glare at him over my shoulder.

Jim looked suitably chagrined.

"Casey took Wolsey down with her," Marie said as she pulled into a parking spot.

"And that's it!" I said cheerfully, opening the car door and hopping out.

"Oh, I don't believe that for a second, my sweet," Jim laughed as he too exited the car. "There's much too much animosity there for a simple fall."

"He did get really muddy," Marie offered, getting out and locking the car behind her.

Jim shook his head. "Uh, uh. Spill!"

I sighed. "He was really angry about getting dirty."

"He would get up and slip and then fall down again," Marie added.

"And I might have knocked him down one more time."

"At least."

"Did we mention we were tipsy?"

"Multiple times," Jim deadpanned.

"Okay, because that's likely why we did what we did next."

Jim raised an eyebrow and waited. We headed towards the hospital entrance.

"We got the giggles," I confessed. "Marie asked him if he wanted to mud wrestle. That was the last straw for him, I think."

"He arrested us," Marie blurted out.

"For being drunk in a public place and..." I coughed and mumbled the rest.

Marie shot me an amused look. "Assaulting a police officer," she enunciated for Jim.

Jim stopped short and stared at us in stunned silence.

Now that the worst of the tale was out, I forged ahead. "He handcuffed us and everything." I still couldn't believe it, all of these years later.

"When we got to the station," Marie explained, "the other cops there took one look at them and asked Wolsey if they'd been mud wrestling."

"I thought he was going to have a heart attack then and there."

"They really laughed at him," Marie added.

"Especially when Marie said something about a pig being happiest in the mud."

"I think that was you."

"Whatever. His co-workers found that hilarious."

"With friends like that..." Marie commented wryly.

"Anyway," I said as we approached the hospital door, "to sum it up, we slept it off in jail instead of at our house."

"You told me at the time that the phones went out," Jim remembered. "And that's why I couldn't reach you."

I shrugged.

"And in the morning the chief let us off with a warning," Marie concluded.

"He told us that we were too OLD for such shenanigans," I complained.

"And Wolsey has had it in for us ever since."

"And vice versa."

We had to stop in the entrance of the hospital to wait for Jim to stop laughing.

We found Stacey McAllister holding court in the visitors' lounge, instead of her room. She was there because a good number of the pipe band members had visited to check up on her. The lounge was the only spot that could fit them all comfortably.

She was propped up on a large, overstuffed recliner, a typical white hospital blanket with a blue stripe at the bottom tucked around her. Although pale, she looked pretty good for someone who had been shot the day before. Her right arm was in a sling and she winced every time she moved. Her auburn curls were bouncier than they had any right to be and her green eyes were alert and indicated intelligence and humour. When we entered the room, she broke into a wide, friendly smile.

"Oh good, more visitors," she called out over the background of numerous conversations being held by a number of people. If I had said those words, they would have sounded sarcastic. But from her, they sounded sincere. Almost as one, the visiting pipe band members stopped talking and turned to check out the newcomers. I spotted Luke, the drummer we had met earlier, and was glad to see a familiar face.

He came forward to greet us and proceeded to make introductions. "Everyone, this is Marie Battler, the editor of the local paper," he began, "here, I presume, to interview Stacey."

At Marie's nod, he continued. "And this is Casey Robertson, a travel writer doing a piece on our town for a magazine, and her husband Jim."

I shot an apologetic smile to Jim for being relegated to 'her husband' status. After many years of being introduced as 'his wife', I knew how that felt.

Luke continued with the introductions. "This brave lady is Stacey," he started. I noticed one woman rolling her eyes. I guess she didn't think getting shot made one brave. "To her left, we have John, Barrett, Kenny, Katie, Charlie, Sara, Gayle, Chuck, Andy, Debbie..."

I tuned out after a few names. There was no way I would remember them all anyway. Besides, I saw Marie writing them all down, so if I needed to recall a name I could just check her list later.

"Nice to meet you all," Marie was saying when I started paying attention again. "I was hoping to ask you a few questions Stacey, if you're up to it."

Stacey smiled that 100 watt smile. "Sure," she agreed. "Do you want to go somewhere more private?"

"I don't mind an audience if you don't," Marie answered.

Stacey nodded and Marie settled into a seat near her. Jim and I drifted away to lean against a wall, still within listening distance but out of the way.

"So, the obvious question is," Marie began, "do you know who shot you?"

Stacey shook her head. "I have no idea."

"Any enemies?"

"No!" Stacey exclaimed. "I try to get along with everyone." She looked sad as she spoke. "I abhor conflict."

Marie nodded in commiseration. I thought I heard someone scoff at Stacey's statement, but when I looked around I couldn't tell where the sound had come from. I glanced at Jim and he raised an eyebrow, indicating that he had heard it as well.

"Were you friends with Matt Lachlan?"

Stacey frowned. "I knew him from band," she said, "but we didn't socialize beyond that." She shuddered. "It was so shocking and sad when he died."

"Were you concerned about piping down the sun after Matt's death?" Marie inquired.

"Mattl," Luke interjected. "We all called him Mattl."

Marie nodded and wrote in her book.

"No, I wasn't," Stacey answered. "Why would we think someone else might be shot? The police said they found the gun that was used."

I leaned over to Jim and whispered in his ear, "The cops found it. Right."

Jim shushed me.

"So, you thought the attack on Matt... on Mattl was...?"

Stacey looked at her fellow band members, then back at Marie. "Personal, I guess?" She made her answer sound more like a question.

"Do you know of any reason someone would have wanted him dead?" Marie continued.

"Well, there have been rumours..."

My ears perked up.

"Such as?" Marie pressed.

Stacey shrugged. "Well, I don't want to speak ill of the dead, but I heard maybe there was an affair..."

"Or something work related," Luke added.

"He could have pissed someone off," one woman offered. I looked to Jim and he whispered "Katie", and I nodded in thanks.

"You never know what goes on behind closed doors," another woman added in a quiet voice barely above a hoarse whisper. Again I looked to Jim, but he was frowning. So much for his help.

"Okay, gossip aside," Marie brought the conversation back on track, "Stacey, did you have anything in common with Mattl?"

Again, the injured woman looked at her band mates, who looked blankly back at her. "Aside from the band, I honestly can't think of anything." She sounded genuinely perplexed.

"Did the police tell you anything about their findings?" Marie asked.

Stacey shook her head and was about to speak when a snarl from the doorway caught everyone's attention.

"No, they most definitely did not!" Wolsey filled the door frame and was already flushed with anger.

"Oh fudge," I muttered.

"I thought I told you to stay out of this?"

The band members looked shocked at his tone. The woman whose name I couldn't remember actually stepped behind a larger man at Wolsey's rough entrance. I wished I could join her, and sized up Jim to see if I could hide behind him. Nope, he was just too skinny to hide behind. I was going to have to start feeding him more.

"You two," Wolsey barked, pointing at Marie and me.

"Three," Jim said.

He was getting the hang of this. I felt a rush of pride.

Wolsey's eyes narrowed. "You THREE," he corrected himself. "Come with me."

He turned and stomped out of the room. We looked at each other, then at the band members. After a second, I shrugged.

"Get well soon," I said to Stacey as I turned to the door. Then, with head held high, I followed Wolsey out of the room, joined by my partner in crime and my partner in life.

As we left, I heard the room behind us explode with conversation. At least we gave them something else to talk about.

"This has to stop!"Wolsey bellowed.

Marie and I put on our innocent faces while Jim took an intense, sudden interest in the ceiling tiles.

"What do you mean De-tec-tive?" I asked sweetly.

"Stop getting involved in this case!"

"We were simply giving Stacey our best wishes..." I began.

"There is nothing simple about the two of you!"

"Three," Jim interjected.

"Awe, thank you De-tec-tive," Marie said at the same time.

Wolsey glared at Jim and ignored Marie, instead sticking his finger in my face, again. If he kept this up, I could end up cross-eyed.

"I don't believe that you went for a simple visit for one second," he growled. "How stupid do you think I am?"

Marie and I both took a deep breath. The glee that I saw in her eyes was surely mirrored by my own. But my darling hubby jumped in to prevent us from following our worst natures.

"Do NOT answer that," he told us, enunciating each word like he was Captain Kirk.

Marie sighed in disappointment. "De-tec-tive," she said. "You know that I have a job to do. I'm required to interview and write about the people who are in the news."

I was shocked to see what looked suspiciously like sympathy, or at least understanding, flash across Wolsey's expression. He switched back to his regular grumpy look so quickly, however, that I was certain I would later be able to convince myself that I had imagined that moment.

"I have a job to do as well," Wolsey declared, scowl back where it belonged. "And I cannot have you two... you three... amateurs getting involved and putting yourselves on a criminal's radar!"

Jim was definitely paying attention now. "Do you have any reason to believe that we are in danger Detective?"

"Well, let me see," Wolsey's voice was full of sarcasm. "You keep turning up, getting involved in the case even when you don't seem to intend to do so." He glared in my direction. "The wrong person could notice that and come to the wrong conclusions."

"And what would those conclusions be, exactly?" Jim asked.

"That you are onto them. That you know who they are." Wolsey paused. "Maybe even that you are following them, since you're the ones finding their discarded weapons. And that would be the wrong conclusion, correct? You have no information regarding these shootings that you haven't shared with the police?"

We looked at each other, and then we all shook our heads in unison. We probably looked like bobble heads.

Wolsey looked a bit disappointed, but that look also disappeared from his face quickly. He reached into his breast pocket and pulled out a card. "If you think of anything... ANYTHING... here is my card." He handed it to Jim. "Call," he ordered.

Jim took the card as I asked, "Like what?"

"Oh, I don't know." Sarcastic Wolsey was back. "How about the name of the shooter?"

"The Piper Sniper?" I quipped.

Marie squealed in glee. "I LOVE that!" She jotted it down in her notebook.

"Do NOT give this criminal a nickname," he growled.

"Too late," Marie sang, waving her notebook at him as she headed for the exit. She was nearly skipping down the hallway; she was so pleased with the moniker. "Come on you two. I have some writing to do. Your ride is leaving."

Jim and I looked at each other, then at Wolsey. Jim smiled apologetically at him, grabbed my arm and practically dragged me out before I could say anything else.

As we exited the building, I looked back to see Wolsey glaring after us, red faced and sweating. At least if he had a heart attack because of our latest encounter, he was already at the hospital.

The Travelling Klutz

A trip to Kincardine in the summer is not complete without participating in at least one Saturday night Pipe Band parade.

The Kincardine Scottish Pipe Band, founded in 1907, draws huge crowds to its weekly parade, which begins at 8 p.m., rain or shine. The band gathers at Victoria Park and marches down Queen Street to Quinn Plaza, where children can bang on the drums and people can meet and chat with the band members. The parade then marches back the way it came, ending up back at the park, where a concert is held for those fans who wish to remain.

The most unique part of this tradition is not the band per se, but those gathered to watch it march. After the band parades by on the street, the crowd steps off the sidelines and joins them, marching behind them to the plaza and then back to the park. It is a sight that leaves many a first time visitor flabbergasted.

With so many people gathered on the main street, it truly is amazing how smoothly the evening goes, week in and week out. Of course, there is always an exception to the rule.

Chapter 13

Jim and I opted for a quiet evening in at the cottage as we had some steaks to throw on the barbecue. And by 'we', I mean 'he', because barbecuing at our house is definitely a man's job - even when that house is a rental cottage.

If truth be told, I don't think Jim trusts me around things that could explode. And that definitely includes propane barbecues.

He took the platter of marinated steaks from the refrigerator out to the back yard while I sliced up some mushrooms into a pan. I added butter and garlic, and while those were cooking I set the table and opened a bottle of red wine to breathe. I returned to the stove to stir the mushrooms and between those stirs I got out a couple of deli purchased salads, a baguette and some flavoured oil for dipping.

Jim stuck his head in the door. "Five minutes, my sweet," he called.

I smiled at his precision. It was one of the reasons we fit so well together. He was meticulous and I was more fly by the seat of my pants. It balanced out well for us.

I spooned the mushrooms into a serving bowl and was placing it on the table when Mrs. Holmberg appeared in the doorway.

"It certainly smells good over here," she said as she walked into the cottage.

"Hello Mrs. Holmberg," I greeted her with a smile. I'd been waiting to see if she would turn up and had only been slightly startled when she appeared.

Jim brought the deliciously aromatic steaks inside. I smiled at the sight of the third steak he had thrown on the barbecue.

"Those smell incredible," I told him.

"Mrs. Holmberg, would you like to join us?" Jim said to the old woman. "I made one for you."

"Oh my, how sweet," she answered, holding a hand to her heart. "But I don't want to invade your dinner time."

"At least let me pack you up a plate to take with you," I offered.

"Well, I couldn't say no to such a wonderful offer," she gushed, looking immensely pleased. I briefly wondered if she'd planned for such an outcome.

I put one of the steaks onto the plate I had set aside and added mushrooms and bread. "Would you like some salad?" I asked her, turning and jumping a little when I found she had silently moved to my side as I worked.

"Oh no, dear," she said, patting my arm, "this is just wonderful. Thank you so much."

Once she'd taken the plate of food back to her home, Jim and I shared a laugh. We were getting used to, and even expecting, Mrs. Holmberg's little visits.

"Thank you for barbecuing," I said to Jim as I sat down at the table. "For all of us."

We've always thanked each other for the things we do, and taught our sons to do the same. We decided years ago that it is important to show appreciation to those closest to you. It's so easy to take your loved ones for granted, when they, above all others, are the ones who deserve your consideration.

He kissed the top of my head as he passed behind me. "Thank you for getting everything inside ready," he answered as he sat down beside me. "And for suggesting we make one for our neighbour. I think she was surprised."

"I'm not so sure about that," I told him. "I think it was her plan all along."

We sat side by side so that we both were facing the large picture window and looking out over the lake. I passed him his Greek salad and I dug into the potato salad, dumping a large spoonful on my plate. A big helping of mushrooms followed, to be joined soon after by one of the medium-cooked steaks.

Jim filled our wine glasses. "To us," he toasted, holding up his glass.

I clinked his glass with mine and took a sip of the wine. When I took a bite of steak, I couldn't help but moan with pleasure. "This is cooked to perfection," I told my barbecue chef.

Jim smiled and took his own bite, nodding in agreement. We were quiet for a while, enjoying our food. After a few bites, Jim paused, looking at me seriously.

"What Wolsey said has me concerned," he told me.

I popped a forkful of steak and mushroom into my mouth, taking the time to consider my answer while I chewed.

"I think he was just trying to scare us," I finally told him.

He frowned. "It's working."

I took a deep breath and let it out slowly. "It's not like we're out there antagonizing people," I protested.

"Except for Wolsey," he pointed out dryly.

I nodded in concession. "He doesn't count."

Jim took a sip of his wine. "He has a point though. You might antagonize the wrong person without even knowing it."

I broke a chunk of bread off and dunked it in oil and herb dip. "Well, how am I supposed to avoid that?" I asked between mouthfuls. "I can't hide away until Wolsey catches the murderer."

Jim smiled at the idea. "Now there's a thought. I'm sure we could find something more interesting to pass the time." He leaned over and kissed my neck, making me giggle.

"We only have a few more days left here," I protested, pushing him away gently. "I need to get all of my photos."

With a sigh, he got up to take our empty plates to the kitchen, I stood and followed, sealing up the salad containers and putting the leftovers into the refrigerator. When I closed the door, he pulled me into his arms for a hug and I snuggled close.

"I know you have a job to do," he conceded. "But can you be a bit less conspicuous while you do it?"

I chuckled. "For you, my love, I will try."

He bent down and gave me a kiss that could still curl my toes. We could probably fit in some of his suggestion for passing the time too. My eyes were still closed when he pulled away. I looked up and met his eyes.

"That is all I ask, my sweet," he said softly.

Saturday dawned bright and clear, the blue sky reflecting on the water and making it even more stunning than usual. We had our coffee out in the back yard chairs, listening to the people walking by on the path between us and the water. Thanks to the bushes on our side of the path, those people had no idea that we were there.

It made for some interesting eavesdropping.

Not that we set out to spy on passersby. Honestly. We were just enjoying the morning - sipping our coffee as we listened to the waves lapping against the shore and the seagulls crying out their calls as they searched for food.

If people are trying to keep their conversations private, they really shouldn't have them in public places.

We heard a couple of male voices approaching on the path from the north. As they got closer to us, their voices became clear. Jim and I recognized the voice of Luke the drummer when he spoke.

"Do you think the parade should be cancelled?" we heard him ask, his voice filled with concern.

He was, of course, referring to the weekly summer pipe band parade. It is attended by hundreds of people almost religiously. People stake out their spots along the route up to an hour ahead of time, while others set up spots in Victoria Park for the concert after the parade. The restaurants and patios along the route do a brisk business before and after the event, making it difficult to get a table on summer Saturday evenings.

Tourists and residents, male and female, young and old, people of every ilk come out to enjoy the parade. When our children were young we were among them, lined up along the route, waiting for the band to go by so we could march along behind them. The boys would be particularly excited at the sight of Blinky, a giant mascot version of the lighthouse, as he walked along just behind the band. Once, our eldest ran to give Blinky a hug and nearly knocked over the poor person inside the costume. Good times.

Back to the weekly parade, Luke had reason to be concerned. To my knowledge it had never, in its hundred or so years of marching, been cancelled. It even went on in the rain.

A female voice, one that sounded familiar but I couldn't place, answered. "It might be safer for everyone."

"But we have NEVER cancelled," Luke argued.

"I said it might be safer, not that I think they'll do it," the woman clarified.

By this time, they had almost reached the cottage and our spot in the back yard.

"Are you scared?" she asked him.

"I'm not a piper," Luke answered. I could see him shrug in my mind's eye. "Whoever is doing this seems to be fixated on the pipers."

"So far."

"Thanks for that." There was a pause. "Are you afraid?"

"I'd be a fool not to be," the woman answered. I realized where I had heard her voice before, now that they were directly behind the bushes that hid us from the path. She was one of the pipers we had met at the hospital when we visited Stacey. "Have you heard if the police are any closer to finding the shooter?" the woman asked.

"All I know is what was in the paper," Luke answered. "They found another gun."

"Didn't that writer woman find both of the guns?"

"Yeah. That's weird, don't you think?"

The voices were almost out of earshot. Now that I was the topic of conversation, I wished they would stop walking and stay closer, so I could hear them better.

"You don't suppose it's her do you? I heard she doesn't like..."

Their voices were now too faint to hear and I got out of my chair to follow them. Jim reached out and grabbed my hand, pulling me down into his lap.

"Uh uh," he admonished. "No following people so you can listen in on their conversations."

"But they think she might be the Piper Sniper!" Mrs. Holmberg's voice reached us from the other side of the bushes.

"You know that's not true, Mrs. Holmberg," Jim called back, not even batting an eyelash at her sudden interruption. "She knows it isn't true, I know it isn't true." Jim rubbed my back to calm me. "Even the police know it."

"But still..." How dare he try to distract me with one of his wonderfully calming backrubs?

"They're afraid," he said softly, as though he expected me to dart like a spooked horse. "Can you blame them?"

"I can," the disembodied voice from next door called.

I laughed and shook my head. "I suppose not. Thank you Mrs. Holmberg."

"You're welcome, dear," she called back. We heard her enter her house as she spoke.

I rolled my eyes and smiled. My next thought sobered me, however. "You don't think the sniper will shoot someone with such a huge crowd there, do you?"

Jim considered the possibility, stopping the backrub as he did. "I don't think so," he answered. I moved to get up from his lap, causing him to tighten an arm around my waist and resume the soothing rubbing of my back. "I really get the impression this has to do with pipers, maybe even the ones at the lighthouse at sunset specifically. There will be too many innocents there tonight. Too much risk."

"I hope you're right," I said softly, and put my head on his shoulder to bask in his attention.

The rest of the day was spent wandering about town (discreetly, as per my handsome hubby's request) and taking photos of various spots the magazine editors might find suitable to include with the article.

We walked south, along the shore of the lake. There was a bit of a breeze, causing gentle waves to break along the shore. Children frolicked in the shallows and a few older kids were trying to catch a wave on their boogie boards. Further out, some teenagers tossed a frisbee back and forth to each other in the water.

I stopped at the Rock Garden, taking a few photos of the tiered cavalcade of colourful flowers. It is a popular spot for newlyweds to take their wedding photos, and I was lucky enough to catch a lovely wedding party doing just that. I went to talk to a woman who I learned was the mother of the bride and she promised to e-mail me the names of the people in the wedding party. Satisfied that I would be able to provide a proper caption should the editors decide to use the photos, I returned to Jim and we continued on our way.

The Pavilion was next on our route and I went to the east side to get a photo of the old dance hall building with the lake in the background. Conveniently, I had been told, the wedding party we had just encountered would be having their reception here later. I had been to a reception there once, and it is an idyllic spot to celebrate nuptials.

We were now walking along the boardwalk. I stopped in front of the five foot tall tree trunk chainsaw carving of a Selkie in Dunsmoor Park. The Selkie, a Scottish mythological creature which lives in the water as a seal and on land as a beautiful woman, sits poised to look out over the waters of Lake Huron. I am always in awe of artists who can create such wonderful pieces. I took a few photos from every angle, and then turned to look in the same direction as the Selkie. I took some photos of the waves rolling over the large breakwall constructed many years ago to protect the harbour.

We continued along the boardwalk until I stopped to take photos of the north side giant blue chairs, again from all angles. These chairs had the added attraction, in my opinion, of being in the shade for much of the day. I took photos of them both with the lake and Tiny Tots Park in the background.

"Aren't you glad to have digital photography?" Jim's question was a subtle dig that I might be taking too many photos.

"No kidding," I answered. "I remember having to limit myself to a roll of film with 24 pictures."

"And you never knew what they'd turn out looking like until they were developed."

I smiled as we reminisced. "Remember when I worked for the Owen Sound Sun Times?" I asked, referring to a larger centre an hour's drive north of us, situated on Georgian Bay. "I used to have to drive the film north to a Port Elgin reporter, who would take it to Alvanley to an editor, who in turn drove it to Owen Sound for the next day's paper."

"That was before we got a modem," Jim recalled.

"I had to read my stories over the phone to someone who would type them there," I added.

"Technology definitely made your job easier," Jim observed. "Of course, it made almost everyone's easier."

I thought a minute before answering. "Unfortunately, it made reporting easier AND contributed to its gradual downfall," I stated. "Now 'citizen reporters' do the job for free and everything is on the internet."

Jim nodded. "Progress waits for no man," he quoted writer Lauren Oliver. "Or woman, for that matter."

At the base of Harbour Street, I took some shots of the flag pole flying the Canadian flag in the gentle breeze, and then we headed for the north pier. When we reached it, I turned east and took some photos of the lighthouse and the marina. As we strolled out onto the pier, I stopped to take photos of the water, the beach, and the town behind us.

Soon we were at the end of the pier. I turned to look north and, due to the beautiful day, was able to see the nuclear power plant clearly on the horizon. I took a few photos and then sat on the edge of the pier, dangling my feet over the waves lapping gently against the concrete. Jim joined me a second later, putting his arm lightly around my shoulders. I rested my head against his shoulder with a sigh.

"I almost don't want to go to the parade tonight," I admitted.

"We can just stay long enough for you to get the photos you need and then go back to the cottage," Jim suggested.

I nodded. "That would be perfect. I'm tired of all the intrigue."

Jim snorted. "You? Really?"

I chuckled. "Well, maybe not the intrigue," I conceded. "But I AM tired of falling down and getting hurt. Not to mention run-ins with you know who."

"And yet you mention it anyway," Jim said sarcastically. We sat quietly for a minute, and then he added, "But I can certainly understand why you'd say that."

We watched the waves as they seemed to reach for our dangling feet. Luckily they missed, because I really didn't want to get my shoes wet.

Jim's stomach broke the silence with a loud rumble. "Want to barbecue some burgers tonight?" he suggested.

"Definitely," I laughed. We got to our feet and started our walk back to the cottage.

We had a dinner of cheeseburgers with all the fixings and leftover salad from our steak barbecue. Oddly, our neighbour did not make an appearance. After cleaning up, we headed down the path towards downtown. There was just enough time to grab a cone at the local ice cream shack before the band was set to march.

I attacked my banana and vanilla double cone with gusto, while Jim took a more measured approach to his adventurous Moose Tracks cone. It consisted of vanilla ice cream with chocolate peanut butter cups and fudge swirled throughout. He would have to do without any kisses from me: I detested the smell of peanut butter, never mind the taste. He knew the rules.

"Could you be any more boring with your choice of ice cream?" he teased.

"Hey, it's not ALL vanilla this time," I protested.

The crowds were starting to gather, even though it was only seven p.m. and the parade didn't kick off for another hour. People had set out chairs on the sidewalks or parked their cars along the route, so they could watch in air conditioned comfort. The stores were enjoying a boost in business as people shopped to pass the time until the parade started or, like us, got a treat to enjoy while they waited. We decided to check out the shops, and wandered in and out of various stores. Or rather I did, while Jim waited patiently outside each store, holding my camera bag.

Shopping just seems to work out better for us that way.

When the street closed to car traffic a half hour before the parade, children took advantage of the chance to play in the middle of the street, running around the road with an abandon that only kids seem to achieve. When I came out of Fincher's, the popular book/toy/gift store and one of the longest operating stores in town, with a book for me and a magazine for Jim, I encountered something I had never seen before in Kincardine.

A protester.

A growing crowd was gathering around an older man at the intersection of Queen and Lambton Streets. The man was bearing a placard and yelling out to anyone who looked willing to listen.

"What's going on?" I asked Jim.

"Some whackadoodle protesting the pipe band!" he answered incredulously.

"Isn't it great?" Marie said gleefully. She seemed to appear out of nowhere and I jumped in surprise when she spoke up beside me. "Come on! Let's check it out!"

We followed her through the crowd, her press credentials parting the people easily. When we got to the front I saw an average looking man wearing all black, a religious white collar clearly visible under his black shirt. He carried a sign that said 'It's big? It's immoral' on one side and 'Gunman sent by God' on the other.

"The pipe band is being punished for its immoral advertising," he ranted at the gathering crowd. "The council members will be next for their 'Pants Optional' vulgarity."

People were starting to yell back at the man in defence of the pipe band, telling him to go away. And those were the nicer comments.

"Is he really with a church here?" I asked Marie.

"I've never seen him before," she shrugged, taking pictures the entire time. "The grapevine has it that he came in from the city."

The yelling had become louder as dedicated fans continued to defend the pipers.

"This could get nasty," Jim observed. As he spoke, uniformed police moved in on the man. The crowd cheered loudly.

But he was not about to go without... well, without protest. He pulled away from the first officer trying to guide him away from the crowd. When another officer blocked his way, the man brandished his sign and swung it at him. The officer deftly ducked out of the way, the sign passing through the air above his head.

Until it came across an obstruction. A collective gasp travelled through the crowd as the sign made loud contact with Detective Wolsey, who was coming up behind the officer who had ducked. He didn't have time to do so himself, and took the sign directly in the head. He was knocked back a few steps and silence descended on everyone gathered.

Impressive, really, considering how many people there were watching the spectacle.

It was quiet enough to hear him grumble what to me sounded like Fred Flintstone's 'frack-n-sack-n-dack-n-black' curse that every kid who grew up in sixties and seventies knew by heart. I don't know what the parents within earshot thought he said, but if looks could kill...

Things went downhill from there. The protester was not in the least bit deterred, and hefted the sign for another swing. Uniformed officers swarmed the man, quickly relieving him of the sign and slapping handcuffs on him. Wolsey stepped forward, his face red from either embarrassment or injury, I wasn't quite sure which, and roughly dragged the protester toward the awaiting squad car.

It was a treasure trove any reporter could only dream of, and Marie was busily taking photos. I don't think I had ever seen her happier, or take photos faster than she did that day.

A cheer rose up from the crowd as the man was led away. When the commotion died down, the first strains of the pipe band faintly reached our ears from Victoria Park at the south end of downtown. People quickly left the street and lined the sides in anticipation, the protester forgotten for the time being. The sound of *Rowan Tree* started to come through loud and clear; the emphasis, of course, on the word loud.

The pipe band was on the march. If neither rain nor a piper sniper stopped them, you can be sure that a wackadoodle protester wouldn't deter them either.

The Travelling Klutz

For many people, the true worth of a place to live lies in its cultural activities. The people of Kincardine are proud of their cultural events, and rightly so.

The Centre for the Arts, located right downtown, is a hub for those activities. The upper floor is home to the Bluewater Summer Playhouse, a professional organization, and the amateur Kincardine Theatre Guild, which runs from fall through spring. The lower floor houses the Victoria Park and Scougall Galleries, highlighting local art and artists, past and present. The adjoining Victoria Park plays host to the Kincardine Scottish Festival and Highland Games, with dancing and concerts staged over the weekend festival. It also hosts the Gathering of the Bands, featuring visiting performers in many genres from Swing to Celtic and everything in between. Other cultural events held in the park include Canada Day celebrations and the Lighthouse Blues Festival's Sunday morning Gospel Revival. The festival itself is held throughout downtown establishments over the course of three days.

The Kincardine and District Secondary School is home base for the Kincardine Summer Music Festival, an excellent two week event that brings in professional musicians to teach participants their craft. The festival spreads out around town with concerts every night in various venues. One of those venues, the Knox Presbyterian Church, has renowned acoustics and also hosts the concerts of the Kincardine Community Singers.

At lakeside Dunsmoor Park you can catch weekly Sunday evening outdoor sing-a-longs with various local musical acts, and Wednesday night Music in the Park featuring the Kincardine Community Concert Band. The Pavilion next door hosts the Lighthouse Swing Band dances, as well as the Artful Hands Show and Sale twice a year.

Rounding out the cultural events are the relatively new Kincardine Pride Celebration parade and meet and greet event, Cruise Night car shows once a month in the summer, and the Through the Garden Gate Garden Tour held by the Horticultural Society.

Something is always happening in Kincardine. The cornerstone of the town's cultural identity is, of course, its Scottish heritage and the pipe band. Be sure to take in the pipe band concert following the weekly Saturday night parade.

You can count on running into the most interesting people.

Chapter 14

The mood among the parade goers was extremely elevated and the approach of the pipers and drummers simply was not enough to explain the party-like atmosphere. Watching a protester get arrested just before the band's march can have that affect on people.

It didn't take long before the general public put two and two together and came to an obvious conclusion. Scuttlebutt on the street as the Scottish band marched along its route was that the police had got their man. By the time the band reached the end of their march, consensus was that the Piper Sniper - yes, that moniker was spreading like wildfire - had been arrested and placed behind bars. And the conclusion that followed was that it was time to party.

Did two and two, in this case, add up to five? Often, the general public could not be bothered with pesky details like evidence or alibis. For this night, the mood took on a celebratory air. People were choosing to believe what they wanted to believe. Everyone was certain that the ordeal was over.

It would be nice, I mused, to believe what the rest of those gathered had happily embraced as the truth. But I had my doubts. Once the band had marched by with its banner bearers and Blinky the walking lighthouse, and those gathered on the street had filed in behind them, I turned to Jim in concern.

"They seem pretty sure that Reverend Whackadoodle is the Piper Sniper," I commented as I watched the people file by in what resembled a conga line more than a parade.

Jim raised an eyebrow. "You're not?"

"Are you?"

"I would like to be."

I sighed. "So would I."

We stared after the marchers as the final notes of *Wings* rang out loud and clear. The pipe band was now holding its weekly meet and greet in the parking lot of Quinn Plaza before back tracking along its route to Victoria Park.

"I just think that if he were really the sniper, why would he draw attention to himself like that with a protest?" I wondered aloud.

"And would a man of the cloth even own a gun?" Jim added.

"Oh please! I knew a priest who went to hunt camp with my father every spring." The memory brought a smile to my lips. Tales of the hunt camp had fascinated both my sister and me when we were kids.

"What?" Jim pretended to be shocked. "Are you implying that men of the cloth are only human?"

I decided that didn't warrant an answer. "So, if all these people are wrong, and Reverend Whackadoodle is not the sniper, that means that the real sniper could be in this crowd somewhere."

We both turned to look north to where we could hear the pipes and drums begin again. The parade was now returning to

Victoria Park for the band's weekly concert in the park. The strains of *Scotland the Brave* were becoming clearer as they approached.

"Surely, you're not thinking you want to go to the concert?" There was a look of trepidation on Jim's handsome face.

"Maybe just for a little while," I admitted. "In such a crowd what could go wrong?" Jim looked alarmed when I said that, so I looked at him mischievously. "And don't call me Shirley."

We waited for the band to pass us, leading what seemed like an endless stream of people to the park. It was like watching a version of the Pied Piper, multiplied tenfold. Only these pipers were being followed by both adults and children, and in much larger numbers.

Once the horde of people danced past us, we fell into line at the back and made our way to the park with them. In all of the years we had lived in town, we had never attended the concert after the parade. I truly was not interested in doing so now either. I just wanted to take a few photos and then wander about to see if anything or anyone looked or sounded suspicious.

The park was crowded with people, almost overwhelmingly so. Those who had remained in the park to reserve the prime viewing and listening spots were being swarmed by the new arrivals. You could tell that those seated and waiting had no idea about the excitement that had taken place down the street. As they were told about the arrest of the protester, they reacted in varying degrees of surprise, amusement, and even shock. I looked around the sea of tartan-clad people with equal measures of interest and bemusement, and settled in to take a few photos. Using my camera's zoom lens

I spotted Mrs. Holmberg in a lawn chair near the centre of the park. So that was why we hadn't seen her at the cottage tonight. I took a photo of her with plans of showing it to her later.

Jim nudged me from behind, leaning to speak into my ear to be certain he was heard over the loud volume of the music on the other side of the park. "Isn't that one of the female pipers over there?" he asked, putting his hands on my waist and turning me so that I was facing in the right direction to see who he was referring to.

I lifted the camera and zoomed in on the woman in question. *A camera*, I mused to myself, *is as good as a set of binoculars*. I recognized the woman as one we had seen at the hospital, part of the group who had been visiting Stacey. She was the one whose ability to hide behind someone to avoid facing Wolsey I'd envied.

"I thought that she was a piper," I stated in puzzlement. "Why isn't she playing with the band?"

I snapped a photo of her, just before she turned to stare in our direction. Hastily, I lowered the camera, immediately feeling foolish for doing so. I was doing nothing wrong.

"I'm pretty sure she's in the band," Jim agreed. "She seemed hoarse when we saw her at the hospital though. Maybe she's too under the weather to play tonight."

I chanced a look in her direction, only to find her still staring at us across the crowd. I had no idea that we were so interesting. Maybe she was just trying to place where she had seen us before. After all, I HAD been taking her picture.

"Why is she staring at us?" Jim asked.

"Let's go say hi and find out," I suggested. "Maybe she has some information to tell us."

We started to weave through the crowd in her direction. We hadn't made much progress when one of the ROMEOs, the Santa look-alike Chris, was suddenly in front of us. He clapped Jim on the shoulder, his broad face beaming a smile at him as if they were long lost buddies. It might have been my imagination, but I thought I saw his belly jiggle like a bowl full of jelly.

"Chris!" Jim greeted him, discretely elbowing me in the side when he heard me snicker.

"Can I pick your brain?" Chris yelled back. I nearly expected him to belt out a 'ho ho ho'.

Jim looked at me questioningly. "Divide and conquer?" he suggested. After all, we'd already learned that ignoring one of the ROMEO's might result in missing out on something important.

I smiled at the old fellow. "Sure. Catch up soon?"

Jim nodded. "You won't have time to miss me," he gushed, planting a quick kiss on my lips.

I smiled at him. "Too late."

Santa Chris was shaking his head. We gave each other another quick peck on the lips, and then I headed for the elusive piper. I noticed that she'd stopped staring at us and I was relieved. It had been getting a bit creepy, truth be told.

I wasn't the least bit concerned about splitting up from Jim. It wasn't like we were in a strange place or didn't know how to get back to the cottage alone if we couldn't find each other. And really, in such a large crowd, what could go wrong?

The Travelling Klutz

I have heard that you can never go home again. We had lived in the small town of Kincardine for almost 30 years. Coming back had been a pleasant experience for us.

As long as you don't count the falls, bumps, bruises, and pulled muscles, that is. Not to mention the two shootings we were witness to. That kind of thing can really put a damper on a visit.

Yes, it had been a nice return trip, and everyone in town had been friendly and welcoming. But, I realized for the first time, it was no longer the place we called home.

That still didn't mean that I couldn't enjoy the visit. And all around me, enjoying their visits was exactly what other people were doing. They were all enjoying each other's company. I planned to do the same. This is a town known for its friendliness, after all.

I should have remembered my favourite John Lennon quote: "Life is what happens when you are busy making other plans."

If you're not careful, death can be what happens too.

Chapter 15

I approached the woman in the park with a bright smile on my face. It did not escape my notice that she regarded my approach suspiciously rather than with anything resembling warmth.

"Hi!" I greeted her with an exaggerated cheerfulness. "Didn't I see you at the hospital the other day?"

She returned my smile with a smaller, more cautious one of her own. "That's right." Then she turned away.

I frowned, thinking that was kind of short of her. "I'm Casey," I ventured.

She turned a rather cold pair of grey eyes on me. "I know who you are."

Okay, this was bordering on plain rude. I looked longingly over at where Jim was clearly enjoying a spirited dialogue with Chris.

"I didn't catch your name," I tried again.

Her gaze got even colder, and I swear I actually shivered a bit, despite the still sweltering heat. "I didn't give it," she snapped.

You'd think that I'd take a hint, but no. That just wasn't my way. Instead, I looked her in the eyes and got into a staring contest. And a staring contest against me is something that this young woman couldn't possibly win. I had lots of practice from my years as a mother, after all.

Finally, she looked away, making a sound in her throat halfway between a sigh and a growl. "Gayle," she spat out her name, refusing to look at me.

I grinned triumphantly at my small victory. That smile faded when I followed the direction of her gaze.

"Is that your husband?" she asked, her gaze firmly locked on Jim across the park. He was looking exceptionally handsome, with his hair tossled, wearing tan shorts and a light, snug shirt that accentuated his strong chest.

I nodded.

"He kind of looks like Kevin Costner," she observed. She swept her cold eyes across me again. "You're an unlikely couple."

Social niceties were clearly not this woman's bailiwick. I chose to ignore the latter part of her statement. "He is handsome," I concurred. Now that we were chatting, kind of, I pressed on. "You seem to be feeling better."

She met my eyes with a puzzled look. "That's an odd thing to say. Why would you say that?"

Now I was puzzled. "I just thought you sounded hoarse when we saw you at the hospital," I explained. When she just shrugged, I opted for a question. "Shouldn't you be over there playing with the band?"

The glare was back. Oops.

"Why? What have you heard?"

I looked at her in surprise. "Nothing," I said hastily. "I just thought you were a piper."

"I'm still in training," she said, bitterness creeping into her voice.

We stood in silence for an uncomfortable minute. An announcement from the band leader interrupted us and we both turned, with everyone else, to see what was going on.

"We would like to welcome back Stacey McAllister," he spoke into a microphone. "She was released from the hospital this morning and, although she will not be playing with us any time soon, we are glad to have her safe and sound in the audience."

The crowd cheered exuberantly and Stacey stood to wave at them with her good arm. Her other arm was in a sling to protect the wounded shoulder. The sling matched her Kincardine Scottish kilt. The crowd's cheers got even louder in response, but quieted quickly once she sat back down and the band began to play its next song.

Gayle was frowning when I turned to look at her. She met my eyes and looked at me as though I had just become interesting to her after all.

"I heard you were investigating the shootings," she stated, asking a question without really asking at all.

"Gosh, I hope Wolsey doesn't hear that," I answered. "He'd toss me in jail and throw away the key." I studied her face. "But, if I were, do you know anything?"

She looked about her furtively, and then moved closer to me. "Maybe," she said, continuing to cast her eyes about us as if afraid of being overheard.

I looked around too. No one was paying any attention to us, including my handsome hubby. I saw him laugh and wished again that I could join him instead of trying to get information out of this grumpy young woman.

"Can I show you something?" Gayle continued.

Now I was interested. I turned away from looking at Jim and gave her my full attention. "Sure," I said cautiously, looking her over in an attempt to see what she might have to show me.

She shook her head. "Not here! It's too crowded." She looked around again, seemingly afraid of being spied on. "At my car."

I frowned. "Where is that?"

She nodded towards the east side of the park. "It's in the old school parking lot."

That wasn't too far, I reasoned. But still... I looked over at Jim again, trying to catch his eye.

"I should let my husband know I'm leaving," I told her, pulling out my cell phone.

"He'll never hear you over all of this noise," she pointed out.

She was likely right about that. "I'll just go and tell him then," I said, starting to move in his direction.

She reached out and caught my arm. I frowned down at her hand and she removed it, stepping back a bit and having enough awareness to look slightly embarrassed.

"You don't need to bother him," she reasoned. "By the time we get through the crowd to him, we could be out to my car and back again."

I studied the crowd. She had another valid point. I waited to see if Jim would look my way, but no such luck.

"Fine," I decided. "But let's be quick."

Gayle nodded and turned to leave. I walked beside her a few steps before asking, "So, what are you showing me?"

"Shhh," she said, putting a finger to her lips and once again looking furtively around at the people we were weaving through. "At the car."

I didn't like being hushed. Frowning, I pulled out my phone again. "I'll just text Jim. It won't take a minute."

Gayle grabbed me by the elbow, guiding me out of the park and across the road with urgency. Thoughts of texting Jim were pushed aside by irritation as we hurried past the old school and over to the parking lot. I didn't like being grabbed any more than I liked being shushed. I tried to yank my arm away, but her grip just got tighter. She was surprisingly strong. I started to protest, but she interrupted me.

"It's just over here."

We approached an orange Volkswagen Bug. Not one of those new, softer versions either - this one was a classic. My boyfriend in high school had driven one of these.

"Punch buggy!" I called, trying to lighten the mood. I delivered a light punch to her shoulder with my free hand.

She let go of me in surprise, glaring at me again.

"What?" I asked. "You've never done that? And you own a punch buggy?"

She shook her head and dug her keys from her pocket. "It's in here," she said, unlocking the door.

"What is it?" I was curious and tried to look around her into the car.

She picked something up from the seat and turned to face me.

"This."

I dropped my phone in surprise. My heart stopped as I looked down at her hands. Then it dropped down into my stomach as I realized that I should never have left the park with her. If I'd just gone over to Jim, she would never have had the chance to point a revolver directly at me.

The Travelling Klutz

When visiting a small town, or a large city for that matter, it is always fun to stroll along the streets, with a friend or on your own. As you stroll, you can check out landmarks, heritage buildings, stores, and other places of interest within the municipality. Strolling is also a good way to get the feel of a place, to greet other people as they pass by, and to get some excellent exercise.

The town of Kincardine is no exception to this. The trail system is not the only enjoyable place for a walk. It is not unusual to see groups of people out walking with walking sticks, or checking their steps on their Fitbits.

There is a very popular self-guided Heritage Walking Tour in the town. In fact, when you pick up the guide, you will see that there are actually six different routes to follow. The first 30 minute walk will take you around Durham Market Square, which surrounds Victoria Park, home base for the iconic pipe band. The second walk also takes about 30 minutes and explores the Queen Street business section. Walk number three will take you 20 minutes and take you past the heritage buildings on Harbour Street, including the lighthouse and the Walker House. The fourth walk, also 20 minutes, will take you from the north pier to Lovers' Lane along the shoreline. Walk five features a 30 minute walk on

Huron Terrace, Lambton Street, and Durham Street, past lovely old residential homes. The 30 minute Princess Street walk is the sixth and takes you to residential homes, and the stately Gothic Revival United Church.

You can wander the more modern parts of town as well. As an added feature that makes a couple of routes in the town more challenging and interesting, the Penetangore River dissects the town, forming a valley that any street running east to west must deal with. Thus, there are two rather steep and large hills to go down and back up when walking those routes.

Of course, those hills become even more challenging when you are walking down one of them with a gun lodged in your back.

Chapter 16

I never understood before why hostages in movies and television shows would meekly go along with whatever their captors demanded, right up until the end of the story or the end of them, whichever came first. Jim would tease me when I yelled at the television screen for the hostage in question to do one thing or the other, to extricate themselves from their predicament.

They never listened to me, of course.

But as Gayle ushered me away from the old school parking lot, past the statuesque Anglican Church at the top of the Russell Street Hill and down the hill towards the bridge, I suddenly understood. It was an epiphany that I would rather not have had at all.

Mind you, I did have the presence of mind to hit the record button for the video feature of the camera I had around my neck as we left the parking lot. At least I listened to me.

"How many guns do you HAVE?" I asked my captor incredulously.

She nudged me from behind with her revolver. "Plenty. I inherited an entire cabinet full of them from my grandfather."

That explains how you could afford to just toss them away, I thought. "Did you kill him too?" I mumbled.

"What did you say?"

"Nothing," I said quickly as I scanned the area looking for a way out of my predicament. I looked at an approaching group of people and thought that things might be looking up.

"Try to get away, try to say ANYTHING," Gayle snarled from behind me, "and one of those innocent people will go with you." She pressed the gun into my back so hard that I winced. That was going to bruise, I knew it. "Maybe even a kid."

Well that was just pure evil. I couldn't help myself, even in this situation, and I pretended to look around. "There are goats? Where?"

She hissed, not appreciating my attempt at humour. "Do you want to be responsible for the death of a kid?"

I shook my head mutely as I watched people, individually or in family groups, walk past us on their way up the hill we were descending. Others went past us going in our direction, in a rush to get home no doubt. I knew in my head that I really would not be to blame if Gayle hurt any of them, that anything that happened next would be Gayle's fault and no one else's. But my heart was not listening to my head at the moment.

Oh, why did I go off without Jim? I wondered miserably. *Why didn't I text him at least?* As we continued down the hill toward the bridge that crossed the river, a more chilling thought occurred to me.

Detective Wolsey had been right. I was going to get myself hurt - or worse. And he had tried to warn me.

I shuddered. Gayle snickered behind me, clearly thinking the shudder was because of her and not my distaste at the thought of Wolsey being right. Regardless, her snicker sent chills down my spine.

"Why are you doing this?" I asked her, falling effortlessly into the part of the hostage, who chats up her captor in an effort to stall in hopes of rescue or escape. I always made fun of that when I watched a television show. The crowd had thinned somewhat, so I felt safe in speaking.

"You were figuring out it was me," she snarled, prodding me with the gun again. That definitely was going to leave a bruise. "I couldn't have you telling anyone."

"You give me too much credit," I protested. Considering that she hadn't really been a suspect in my books, I wasn't lying. "But I promise that I won't tell anyone now," I added, a little too desperate sounding to my own ears.

"That's right, you won't."

We were crossing the bridge. I looked over the railing at the rushing water far below and wondered if she was going to push me over the railing. A family passing us by likely saved me from that fate. They nodded at us, smiled, and continued up the hill, no doubt oblivious to what was going on around them in their rush to get home and put the kids to bed.

How DID we miss her as a suspect? I wondered. "But why would you shoot those pipers?" I asked out loud.

We were at the other side of the bridge by now and she pushed me across the road towards the trail access on the opposite side. From there I knew, as surely as if she had told me outright, that her plan was to force me to go through the grassy area where Scouts used to camp and under the bridge. Even if Jim had noticed that I was gone, would he find us there? I had to keep stalling, I realized. So I tried to get her to talk again.

"Why did you do it?" I asked again.

We reached the bottom of the hill and Gayle pushed me towards the path that led under the bridge. Sometimes I really hated being right.

"Why? I'll tell you why! It should have been ME!"

My eyes widened in realization. It all suddenly made sense. This was the woman whom Jim had overheard that first night, complaining about Mattl getting special treatment. This was the same woman who had knocked me over with a door at the old town hall. When we had seen her at the hospital, she had retreated behind another piper and pretended to have a sore throat, so we wouldn't recognize her or her voice. Despite the danger, I had to confirm my new suspicions. I pretended to look confused as I dared to turn and stare into her eyes. Her face was red with anger and she looked crazed.

"I don't understand," I said, playing the confused bystander for all it was worth.

"Piping down the sun!" she exclaimed. "It should have been me! Neither one of them deserved it!"

Well there you have it, I thought. I was now very pleased with myself that I had hit record on the camera earlier. There would be evidence of her confession even if I didn't make it. But I was still on the lookout for a way out. Or to be rescued. I wouldn't be averse to playing the damsel in distress right now. I had to keep stalling.

"This is about you getting to pipe down the sun?" I asked incredulously.

"Mattl had moved away," she snarled. "He shouldn't have taken the spot. He just did it to show off. And Stacey..." She spat the other woman's name as if it were the most distasteful thing she had ever said. As if she had not threatened to kill children a few minutes ago. "She started with the band at the same time that I did, but SHE got chosen over me."

I tried to look sympathetic while also trying to send a telepathic message to my husband. *Come find me, we're under the Russell Street bridge.* I don't think either attempt succeeded, but I had to try.

"That sucks," I ventured, but it came out too much like a question.

Gayle glared at me. She definitely had anger issues. "They said that SHE was a natural and that I had to practice more." She pushed the gun into my side and motioned me onto the path in front of her. I stumbled slightly, but reluctantly started to move. I did take my precious time about it though.

"They said that I wasn't good enough." She let out a sinister laugh. "I showed them."

I didn't see the connection. "How does killing a man and injuring a woman show them that you have talent?" I asked without thinking.

If looks could kill, I would have been dead a few times over. I shivered at the cold glare I saw when I glanced over my shoulder. Or perhaps it was at the general chill creeping into the air now that the sun was almost gone. She pulled me to a stop and pointed down a sharp incline in the path. It went down towards the water of the river before making a sharp left. At that point, the path followed the water under the bridge.

Under it and completely out of sight from above. Right where I definitely did not want to go.

"You don't have to do this," I pleaded, fear creeping into my voice.

"Yes I do."

"You don't want to though," I suggested, trying some reverse psychology.

"Actually, I think that I do," she sneered at me.

She pressed the gun into my side again and gave me a small push. *Two bruises*, I amended in my head.

She clearly didn't know who she was dealing with though, shoving me like that. Not because I was brave or skilled in self defence or any other athletic prowess that might be helpful in this situation. No, she was not taking into account that she had kidnapped a klutz.

Or that shoving said klutz at the top of a sharp incline could not end well.

I slipped, of course I slipped, my feet going out from under me. As soon as I lost my footing, all thoughts of that gun went out of my head in favour of my more immediate danger to, if not life, limb. I was not getting any younger, after all. And I had already fallen down way too many times this week. My arms pin wheeled back towards her as I attempted to save myself.

One of my arms came down at full speed on Gayle's. The force of the blow pushed the hand holding the gun down, away from my flailing self, and towards the ground.

Two things happened almost simultaneously: Gayle accidentally shot the gun into the ground, and she slipped. Her finger had been on the trigger; she really had been prepared to shoot me! We were so close to the underside of the bridge that the sound reverberated loudly, leaving my ears ringing.

Surely someone heard that, I thought.

What followed seemed to happen in slow motion. The hand holding the gun rose as she tried to save herself from falling, much the same way I had a few seconds earlier. As she fell, her finger squeezed the trigger again. I swear I felt the bullet whiz by my head as it headed towards the underside of the bridge, leaving my ears ringing even louder than before.

Luckily I was on my way down the hill at that point. Otherwise I could very likely have been shot in the head. I hit the ground with a thud. Gayle followed quickly behind.

Amazingly, I finally found myself in a situation in which I had some expertise. As I thudded to the ground, I rolled sideways down the hill, cradling the camera as I did so. The roll absorbed the excess energy and took me out of the way of my falling captor.

Gayle crashed to the ground, landing with an audible thud on her butt. Clearly not being an experienced, let's say tumbler, she fell backwards and cracked her head on the hard ground behind her. It might actually have been a rock that she hit, judging by the sickening sound that I heard when it happened. It was a crack, like the breaking of a nut out of its shell at Christmas. As I came to a stop, I watched the gun fly out of her hand and land a metre or so away in some tall grass. She slid down the hill towards me on her back, feet first, and I scrambled out of the way in case she had a quicker recovery time than I usually did and pounced on me. I need not have worried. She didn't so much as budge once she stopped sliding down the embankment.

Which is a shame because I was hoping her momentum might carry her right into the fast flowing river. Not nice of me, I know, but to be fair, she HAD been planning on killing me.

The sound of pounding feet against the ground above me made me look up the incline we had just tumbled down.

"We came to rescue you!" Jim called, skidding to a stop. He took in the sight of me sitting on the ground in front of a prone and unconscious Gayle with clear surprise on his face. "Not that you seem to need it," he concluded.

Behind him a group of huffing and puffing ROMEOs stared at me in amazement. I'm fairly certain that my look matched theirs as I took in their breathless arrival.

"Thanks," I said, completely sincere but still a tad bit sarcastic.

Then I eased my newly aching body back onto the ground and breathed a sigh of relief. I was going to have more than a few new bruises after this ordeal.

The Travelling Klutz

There is a universal truth when it comes to living in small communities. No matter where in the country, or the world, you are, if you live in a small community, you can count on two things.

The first is that any news involving you will become common knowledge with astonishing speed. The community knows it before the community news organizations do. I dare you to try tracking the dissemination of this news. I have yet to find anyone who has been able to follow the tangled web that is the community grapevine.

This phenomenon has been going on for as long as people have lived in groups, long before social media outlets such as Facebook and Twitter came about, making sharing news virtually instantaneous. Yet the little old lady down the street who could never be bothered to go online or get a cell phone will know the news before anyone else. How that is actually achieved remains one of the great mysteries of our time.

The second truth of small town living is that, should you need help, you can count on getting it. You will, in fact, likely get more help than you need, or want. And that help will more than *likely be unsolicited. By the time you think to ask for aid, there is a queue of people ready and willing to offer it.*

Now there is a train of thought that people in the community offer to help so that they can get more information to spread on the grapevine. That would create a circular relationship between the spreading of news, otherwise known as gossip, and the giving of aid to those about whom the news refers.

That's the word on the street anyway.

Chapter 17

The ROMEOs stood guard over the unconscious Piper Sniper, the four of them resembling the horsemen of the apocalypse in the twilight as they surrounded her, while we waited for the police to arrive. Jim stood guard over me.

"I've never been so happy to see you as I was tonight," I told him as he held me close. "Well, maybe when I saw you waiting at the end of the aisle on our wedding day, but the two times might be tied." His gentle squeeze was his only acknowledgement of my statement. I was beginning to think that he would never let me go.

Flashlights lit up the increasingly dark evening as the police approached from where they'd parked their cruisers on Russell Street. We'd seen their cruisers speed down the hill, flashing lights piercing through the dark as they sped to the closest spot that a vehicle could reach. The officers left the lights on when they left the vehicles and started walking towards us. They were followed by an ambulance, also with its lights flashing.

A lone flashlight approached from the trail to the north. I wiggled out of Jim's arms, ignoring his protest, and squinted towards that light. Soon I could make out Marie jogging towards us in an attempt to arrive before the police did. She must have parked on Durham Street and taken the trails between the two streets. That wasn't a hike I'd have wanted to take in the dusk. Then again, Marie had always been much more coordinated than I was. The triathlon training suddenly made more sense.

"You called her?" I looked questioningly at Jim. He just smiled and shrugged. I hugged him tightly. "You're a good guy."

"Don't forget that," he murmured and kissed the top of my head.

Marie stormed onto the scene, nodded to us, and immediately began taking photos. The ROMEOs stepped back to give her a clear shot of the unconscious Gayle, then resumed their positions. They were taking their guard duty very seriously. When she had a few pictures, she smiled in thanks to Jim, and then turned to me.

"You okay?"

"I've had worse falls," I answered.

"Recently," Jim muttered, prompting Marie to chuckle.

She stared for a few seconds at Gayle's prone form, and then spared a glance at the ROMEOs. I seriously wondered what the old guys would do for excitement once Jim and I left town.

"Never a dull moment, eh?" Marie asked them.

As if to prove that very point, Wolsey slid down the embankment Gayle and I had just tangled with and lost. I held my breath in anticipation, but he clearly had better balance than I have and stayed, sadly, on his feet.

"I TOLD you that sticking your nose where it doesn't belong could put you in danger," he scolded me.

The last thing I needed was for him to tell me 'I told you so'. "I'm fine. Thank you for asking, De-tec-tive," I snapped. I didn't really mean to, but I was getting tired and sore. It just came out.

Wolsey may have looked a little chagrined, but it was dark, so I might have imagined it.

"Smile De-tec-tive," Marie teased. "You've got your Piper Sniper."

Wolsey scowled at her. "I AM smiling," he muttered, drawing an amused chuckle from Jim and the Romeos.

The ambulance attendants arrived and the ROMEOs stepped away from their guard duty. Gayle was carefully placed onto a backboard and strapped in, then quickly put onto a litter and carried up the hill. The paramedics wanted me to go to the hospital too, but for once Wolsey and I were on the same side.

"I'll be interviewing her down at the station," he told them. "If she needs medical attention, we'll do first aid there and then bring her to the hospital ourselves."

The paramedics seemed satisfied with that arrangement and we all trekked up the hill to the street. I was getting stiffer by the second and leaned heavily on Jim. The ambulance went one way while the ROMEOs, Jim, and I got into a couple of police cars for the trip to the station. Marie stayed behind with the crime scene investigators to see what she could find out at that end.

"Keep me posted," she whispered to me as we passed her on the trail.

I gasped and turned to Jim. "I dropped my phone," I told him, trying to keep from sounding like a little girl who had lost her favourite toy. I'm pretty sure I failed.

Jim pulled the device out of his pocket and handed it to me. "I called it and found it by following the ring tone," he said. "By the way, my ring tone is Darth Vader's theme?"

I giggled, a bit too hysterically, as I took the phone from him and pocketed it. Ignoring his question, I gave him another hug. "My hero," I whispered in his ear.

We all sat around a large conference table at the police station. I was relieved that we hadn't been split up into individual rooms for the interviews.

In the light of the police station, it became clear that I hadn't come out of the ordeal unscathed. My clothes were muddy and grass stained. There were twigs tangled in my hair that Jim helped wrestle out of the curls. My cheeks were tear stained, and I quickly wiped them in hopes that no one had noticed. I had numerous scrapes and cuts that needed cleaning and dressing. In fact, I was sure that I resembled a mummy, as the officer who had given me first aid had been quite zealous with the white bandages. Fortunately, the time the first aid took had the benefit of allowing me to make some sense of my disjointed thoughts before facing Wolsey.

Once in the conference room, the ROMEOs - Norm, Larry, Chris, and Andrew - took up one whole side of the large table, while Jim and I sat close together on the other side. Wolsey sat at the head of the table, pen and paper at hand, ready to begin the questioning.

"This should be interesting," Jim muttered.

"I think you have a new catch phrase," I teased him, leaning against his shoulder for emotional support.

"Alright," Wolsey began. "Let's start at the beginning."

They all turned to look at me. I took a deep breath, and explained how Jim and I had noticed Gayle staring at us in the park. I added that I had gone to find out what she found so interesting, while Jim stayed behind to talk to the ROMEOs. Then I took them through her odd mood swings, our trip to the parking lot, and the moment she pulled a gun on me.

"That's when I hit record on the camera," I said, sliding the memory card across the table to Wolsey.

"Good thinking," he said.

I almost fell out of my chair. Which would have been embarrassing, because I had already fallen out of one chair this week. I took a sip of water from the glass in front of me to hide my shock at the compliment.

I continued with my statement, taking them through the walk to the trail and finally my accidental tripping up, literally, of my captor.

The ROMEOs exploded with laughter. I saw Wolsey's lips lift slightly at the corners of his mouth and I thought I heard him mutter something that sounded a lot like 'I know how she felt'. But again, I could have imagined it. I was getting more exhausted by the minute.

Jim grinned indulgently at me. "Only you," he said, reaching over and squeezing my hand.

Eager to get the attention off me, I turned to Jim with my own questions. "And then you were there," I said. "How did that happen? Did you get my telepathic cry for help?"

He looked at me, clearly puzzled. "Uh, no?"

Wolsey cleared his throat and we all turned to him again.

"So, Mr. Robertson, how did you and your..." he searched for the right word. "... comrades end up at the scene?"

Jim took a deep breath to take up the tale where I had left off. But before he could say anything, he was interrupted by Chris.

" ROMEOs," he said glibly.

Wolsey frowned at him. "Excuse me?" Clearly he had more respect for his elders than he did for reporters or writers.

" ROMEOs," Norm jumped in. "Not comrades. We are the ROMEOs." He waved his hand around to indicate the three other men and himself.

"Really Old Men Eating Out," Andrew explained.

"You can join the club soon if you like," Chris added.

Wolsey was starting to look vexed. It was amusing to watch when I wasn't the cause. Jim came to his rescue and I felt like kicking my husband under the table. I refrained, because he really didn't deserve it.

"I was talking to the ROMEOs. When I looked over to check on Casey, she was gone."

"He panicked," Norm interjected.

"I did not panic."

Larry held up his index finger and thumb and said, "A little bit, you did."

I giggled, oddly pleased to hear that Jim had been upset at my absence.

"Norm spotted Casey and Gayle crossing the road on the far side of the park," Jim continued, opting to ignore not only the two of them, but my impersonation of a teenage girl as well.

"The lad took off like a shot!" Norm added.

Wolsey and I both frowned, wondering who the lad was, where he had come from, and how he fit in.

"They mean me," Jim explained.

Wolsey was starting to turn red, but he kept writing down everything he heard.

"By the time we got to the school, the women had already left the parking lot," Jim continued. "I tracked down Casey's phone, which I'd really hoped she had on her. We made our way to the street and kept asking people if they'd seen the two of them."

"Which slowed us down quite a bit," Norm grumbled.

"Eventually we were directed down the hill," Jim continued.

"Once we got to the bridge, it was pretty clear where Gayle would be taking Casey," Andrew added.

"Then we heard the first shot." Jim visibly shuddered and I reached over and squeezed his hand. I was not giggling any more. Mostly I felt bad that I had giggled at all.

"We got to the field and then there was a second shot," Jim said quietly, taking my hand in his and holding it tightly. "I feared the worst."

Larry picked up the tale. "When we got there, both of the ladies were on the ground. We took up positions around them, and called you."

"And that's how you found us," Andrew concluded the tale.

Wolsey took pity on us not long after that and had some officers take us back to the cottage. Where the ROMEOs went I have no idea. I suspect it may have been to the coffee shop to celebrate their adventure.

We had barely set foot inside the door and turned on the lights, when we heard a knock on the door.

"Go sit down and relax," Jim urged me. "I'll get it."

I settled onto the cozy, overstuffed couch with a relieved sigh. He opened the door to find Luke and Stacey. She was carrying a pizza box in her free hand and he held up a six pack of Molson Canadian.

"We just wanted to make sure you were okay," Luke said. "We won't be staying."

"I thought you might be hungry," Stacey added, shoving the pizza box into a confused Jim's hands and pushing past him. She came over to me, sat down beside me and leaned in to give me a big hug.

"Thank you so much!" she said. "You caught her! I feel so much better now."

I gently pried her off me. Much more squeezing and I would get more bruises. "Actually, I think she caught me, but you are very welcome."

"Maybe we could all get together for lunch tomorrow?" Luke suggested, pulling Stacey away from me and towards the door.

"That would be nice, as long as Casey is up to it," Jim said, as he walked them out. I heard the conversation continue, no doubt to arrange the lunch details, as they walked towards the path behind the cottage. I opened the six pack and took out two beer, opening one and taking a large swig before opening the pizza box to check out our bounty.

I heard voices returning. That wasn't right. Jim should be alone.

He came in followed closely by a tall, slim, blonde girl dressed in a flowing skirt and loose fitting T-shirt. After a moment I recognized her: she worked behind the counter at the coffee shop. I didn't even know her name, and here she was on our doorstep.

On our doorstep bearing a box of baked goods.

"All of us at the bakery just wanted to bring you a treat to enjoy after the difficult evening you've had," she said.

I looked at her in surprise. "How did you know about that?"

She shrugged. "The ROMEOs were in."

Of course they were, I thought.

"How are you feeling?"

"If there are vanilla cupcakes in there, I would say things are looking up," I joked.

She smiled and nodded. "We know what you like," she said, surprising me again. I didn't realize that my unhealthy snacks were common knowledge. Still, who was I to turn down cupcakes?

"That is so sweet ... I'm sorry, I've forgotten your name."

"This is Brittany," Jim told me before turning back to her. "Thank you so much for stopping by."

She nodded, her long bangs falling briefly into her eyes. She must have known she was being rushed out but didn't seem to mind. "Well, I hope to see you at my work soon. Enjoy the cupcakes."

Jim walked her out and returned quickly. He looked at the food on the table in bemusement.

"Quick, turn out the lights," I suggested. "That way any other visitors will think we've gone to bed early."

"Good idea," Jim said, reaching over to the light switch. He yelped when his hand came down on top of a smaller one.

"Mrs. Holmberg! You startled me!"

"Sorry about that," she said, not appearing to be at least a little bit sorry. She held up a jar and waved it in the air as she crossed over to me. "I brought you some liniment."

"Oh you didn't need to..." I began.

"Shush," she said, sitting beside me on the couch. "I make this myself for my own aches, and it works wonders for me."

She had a point there. If I could come and go anywhere near as quickly as she did, I'd be ecstatic. Perhaps this was her secret weapon.

She opened the jar. It looked like Vaseline and smelled suspiciously like Tiger Balm or Vicks VapoRub. "It's an old family recipe," she told me. "Just get your handsome man here to rub it on your aches before bed." She moved her eyebrows up and down. "But I can't be held responsible for what might happen afterwards."

"With that smell, I don't expect it would be much, including sleep," Jim muttered. We laughed at him, and I thanked our neighbour for her thoughtfulness.

She patted my hand and rose to go. "Thank you, dear. You ferreted out a killer." She crossed to the light switch and flipped it to the off position, plunging us into darkness. "To keep the visitors away." We heard her chuckle as the door closed behind her.

Jim locked the door, and then made his way over to me in the dark. I handed him his beer.

"It was awfully nice of them all to come by," I said, closing Mrs. Holmberg's jar and helping myself to a slice of deluxe pizza.

The Travelling Klutz

You always know when you have had a good vacation if, when it comes time to leave, you are a little reticent to do so.

What kind of a vacation leaves you with that feeling? A vacation to a place where the people made you feel welcome and left you with warm memories. A vacation to a place that had plenty of natural beauty, resulting in numerous scenic photos with which to commemorate the visit. One with plenty of things for you to do, leaving you with sore muscles and tall tales as evidence.

For some it is a place with interesting and unique shopping experiences. For others it is the cultural experiences that make for a memorable vacation spot. It could be the culinary tastes and aromas that stick in your head. Beaches and water sports are also high on the lists of top experiences for travellers.

The town of Kincardine has all of those things in one small little package. Perhaps that is why they say the town is the place where you are only a stranger once; because after that first visit you feel like you have left a part of you there. So when you return it is a little like returning home. And you are always up for a return visit.

Even when your last visit was much more... let's say, exciting... than most.

Chapter 18

We'd taken over a large part of Gilley's patio, combining a few tables into a larger, rectangular one. The sun was beating down and people passing by on the street showed signs of exasperation, and perspiration, in the oppressive midday heat. But in our spot, sheltered by the branches of the massive, centrally located maple tree, we were quite comfortable.

Marie sipped from her spicy Caesar, pulling the stalk of celery out of the glass and crunching down on it with zeal. I wrinkled my nose in mock disgust.

"Vegetables do not belong in cocktails," I grumbled.

My old friend rolled her eyes at me dramatically. "Tomatoes are fruit," she argued.

"Celery isn't." I took a big swig of my ice cold lager. "Then again, I'm not sure celery qualifies as food at all."

Marie shrugged. "That's quite a bruise on your shin," she noticed, pointing to my leg.

I looked down at the yellow mark on my shin. "It's getting better actually," I said. "It's from when I ran into the picnic table and fell onto the bench."

Mrs. Holmberg sat between me and Marie, drinking a glass of red wine and listening intently to the conversation. "I remember that," she chuckled.

I looked at her in surprise, but decided not to comment. Of course shed seen that mishap, even though we hadn't noticed her presence at the time. Instead I pulled up the sleeve of my new 'Pants Optional' t-shirt to reveal another bruise on my shoulder. It was a large, yellowing, black smear across my skin. "This is from when I fell in the forest."

Both women winced in sympathy. I continued, standing and turning my back to them. I lifted my shorts slightly. "And this black and blue bad boy is from being bowled over by a door," I explained.

"That was funny!" Marie told Mrs. Holmberg.

I let out a put-upon sigh, causing them both to laugh. I turned to show them a purplish mark on the side of my right leg. "This one is from falling off the big blue beach chair."

"Only you could fall from a sitting position," Marie observed.

I ignored her and turned around again, lifting my t-shirt to expose the small of my back. "This is from having a gun rammed repeatedly into my back." I was actually assuming there was a bruise there, since it was tender to the touch. I hadn't actually checked in the mirror.

They both sobered and winced in sympathy.

"And last but not least," I faced them again and pointed to both of my knees, which were scraped and raw, with bruises just beginning to show up around the edges of the raw skin. "These are from my tumble down the hill under the Russell Street Bridge."

"Those are all definitely impressive dear," Mrs. Holmberg said, leaning over and patting my hand as I eased back down into my chair.

I smiled warmly at her. "Thank you," I said. "It's nice to be recognized."

Marie rolled her eyes, but anything she might have said was sidelined as Jim arrived with all of the Romeos in tow. They had gone inside to the bar to get refills of their beer. Jim sat beside me, taking a sip of his reddish beer as he did so, and the Romeos fanned out on the far side of the table. Norm took the spot at the head of the table next to Jim, I assume in order to have the best listening spot.

Not long after, Stacey joined us from where she'd gone to wait for Luke at the entrance to the patio. She sat down across from Marie. She'd insisted on buying the first round of drinks, as a gesture of thanks for us rooting out her assailant. Despite delivering that delicious pizza the night before, she still seemed to think she owed us something. I made sure to thank her profusely.

Luke, who hadn't been there for the first round, came out of the bar with a pint of beer in hand and took the seat between Stacey and Andrew. Marie and I exchanged a knowing glance when Luke and Stacey shared a fond, lingering look. He was heaping attention on the lovely piper and we were certain there was a budding romance happening before our eyes.

News of our exploits had made the rounds in town quickly and people were even more friendly to us than they had been before, if you can imagine that. Marie's story in the paper had drawn much more attention to us than we would have liked, but the ROMEOs had no such qualms. They were good to have around, as they were basking in the attention and running interference between us and well-wishers. We were glad to have them save us from the excess of attention.

"When are you heading back?" Marie asked.

"Tomorrow," I answered.

"I'll miss seeing you each day, dear," Mrs. Holmberg said as she patted my hand warmly.

"We need a vacation from our vacation," Jim quipped, drawing good natured laughter from everyone around the table.

"It may have been a vacation for you, but I was working," I pointed out.

"Is that what you call it?"

I cuffed him lightly on the back of the head.

"If looking after you is what you call a vacation," he continued, "maybe I should stay home next time."

My pout brought more laughter from the table.

"Speaking of work," Stacey segued, "were you able to get your article finished?"

I chuckled. "Surprisingly, yes I did. I finished it late last night and sent it off to my editor this morning. Along with way too many photos, I might add."

"She gave me a wonderful photo she took of me at the concert," Mrs. Holmberg gushed.

The waitress returned and we placed an order of various appetizers for the group to share 'family style'.

"So Stacey, did you have any suspicions about Gayle?" Norm called from the head of the table once the waitress had gone to deliver our order to the kitchen.

Stacey looked at Luke and they simultaneously shook their heads. "Not really. I knew that she was jealous of me," she said, "because we joined at the same time and I was doing better and getting along with people easier than she was. But I never in a million years would have thought that she could be violent."

"All of us in the band think of each other as family," Luke added, putting an arm around Stacey's shoulders and giving her a comforting squeeze. "It's been quite a shock. It's like your little sister went all serial killer at the family reunion."

"Oh, like family eh?" Marie teased. "So you and Stacey are like brother and sister then?"

They both turned red with embarrassment. "Well, not all of us are like siblings," Luke mumbled, removing his arm from Stacey's shoulders.

I took pity on them. "I can imagine that it's been quite stressful," I sympathized. I turned to Marie. "Any idea what Gayle has had to say for herself? Or should I be asking the ROMEOs instead?"

Marie shot me a dirty look and was about to answer when we heard a masculine clearing of the throat behind us. We turned and looked up to find Detective Wolsey standing there listening.

"You should be asking me," he growled.

"Oh no," I groaned.

"We didn't do it," Marie told him quickly.

"Do what?"

"Whatever you're here to yell at us about."

He snickered. It was so close to a laugh that I looked to Jim to see if he had heard it too. He just shrugged and drank from his pint. I followed his lead.

"I saw you from the street and wanted to see how you were doing." Wolsey seemed to be directing the statement at me.

I stared at him for a moment, and then looked over my shoulder. Maybe he was speaking to someone behind me.

Nope, no one else was there.

"Me?" I squeaked.

Wolsey sighed, showing a bit of the frustration we had come to expect from him.

"Would you like to join us Detective?" Jim asked. Nine heads swivelled to look at him in surprise.

Wolsey paused briefly. "Don't mind if I do," he decided, pulling up a chair at the foot of the table, directly opposite Norm, and between Stacey and Marie.

Our heads all swivelled from Jim to Wolsey, before settling on the detective with varying looks of shock. Where had this sociable person come from and what had he done to the cantankerous detective?

The waitress arrived with a tray loaded with food, accompanied by another staff with a second large tray full. There were deep fried potato skins with cheese and bacon, my favourite garlic bread with cheese, escargot, mushrooms topped with a crab mixture, deep fried pickles, original and chili cheese nachos, onion rings and fries, and four different flavours of chicken wings. Basically, we'd ordered at least one of everything on the appetizer menu. Once the food was placed in the centre of the table and we all had plates, she took our drink refill orders.

"And for you sir?" she asked Wolsey.

"I'll have a pint of Guinness," he answered. Seeing our stunned looks, he added, "What? I'm off duty." He sounded a little defensive to me.

"So Detective," I began, deliberately refraining from dragging the word out as we'd been doing all week. If he could be nice, the least I could do was try to follow suit.

"Ed," he interrupted.

The shocks just kept coming. "What?"

"My name is Ed," he said. "Off duty. No need for formalities." He took a long drink from his pint the second the waitress put it in front of him.

It had never occurred to me that he had a first name. "Uh, okay. Ed." It really felt weird saying that. The ROMEOs were snickering at my obvious discomfort and I cast a glare in their direction. "How is your prisoner doing?"

Was that mischief dancing in Wolsey's... I mean Ed's eyes? I looked at Marie, who seemed as stunned as I was. Actually, I decided that this version of the detective SHOULD have a different name. He was that different from the person we had come to know and antagonize.

"I cannot discuss an ongoing investigation," Ed deadpanned.

"But you said we should ask you!"

He laughed. Actually laughed! "I'm just yanking your chain," he said. "She came to with quite a headache."

"That happens when you tangle with Casey," Jim muttered.

"Don't I know it," Wolsey groused. "Anyway, the doctor said she has a mild concussion. And off the record..." He shot a warning look at Marie, who nodded after a moment of consideration. "... she's trying to say she didn't do it."

Jim choked on a bite of garlic bread. I slapped him on the back helpfully.

"She TOLD me she did it," I protested between slaps. "I got a recording of her telling me she did it."

The back blows got more aggressive with each word I spoke, resulting in Jim turning and gently grasping my hand in mid air. "I'm good now sweetheart," he teased.

Ed bit into a chicken wing and nodded. "That you did," he agreed with me. "But she doesn't know about that yet."

"Do you think she'll try for an insanity defence?" Marie asked.

Ed sighed. "Your guess is as good as mine," he told her. "But I wouldn't be surprised. All I have to do is gather the evidence though. I leave the rest up to the lawyers and the court."

"But she's guilty!" Stacey exclaimed. The colour in her cheeks seemed to have drained away. "She can't get off without punishment! Can she?" She turned increasingly pale as she spoke and took a big gulp of her wine, finishing off the glass.

Larry, who was heading inside for a visit to the little boys' room, patted her shoulder as he passed behind her to get to the door. "Trust in the system," he said. "She'll get what's coming to her."

It occurred to me that I had no idea what Larry, or Norm for that matter, had done for a living before they retired. Maybe Larry had been a lawyer. The other two, younger ROMEOs - younger being a relative term - were the ones Jim knew from the plant, but I didn't know what they had done there either.

Then Larry shot a sultry smile in Mrs. Holmberg's direction. I looked in shock at our temporary neighbour, only to see her returning his smile. And was she blushing? I glanced at Marie to see if she had seen that as well. She nodded at me, a smile pulling at the corner of her lips. There were apparently two budding romances in our little group, and at opposite ends of the age spectrum.

We were all quiet for a while, enjoying the food, drink, and companionship.

"Speaking of evidence..." I began.

Ed frowned. "Aren't you due to leave?" he asked.

"Tomorrow," Jim answered.

"Not a moment too soon," Ed muttered.

"What was that?"

"What?"

"You said something."

"No I didn't." He stuffed the last bit of a deep fried pickle in his mouth.

"Yes. You did."

"Speaking of evidence," Marie pressed.

"Stay out of it," he warned.

"If you need any help," she offered.

His eyes narrowed. "I'll call her," he said, pointing at me.

The table exploded into laughter. Who knew he could be funny if he tried?

"Casey will not be falling over or into any more of your evidence, Ed," Jim assured him.

"So where will you go and write about next?" Luke deftly changed the subject.

I pretended to consider the question when I really knew the answer, sipping my beer for dramatic effect. After a moment, I let them in on my plans. "I'm thinking, since fall is approaching, Port Elgin would be nice to visit during Pumpkinfest."

The table exploded into conversation, and I heard variations of 'great idea', 'that is so close by' and 'we could join you', which made me smile.

I looked around at all of the people sharing food and drink with us. A week ago I wouldn't have imagined such a warm gathering with such a diverse group of people. Today I was saddened, knowing I would have to say goodbye to them all.

Jim, as usual, picked up on my train of thought. "We'll be back," he reminded me.

"We will?"

"You will?" a chorus of voices repeated.

Ed sighed. "They have to come back to testify at the trial," he clarified.

"Unless she pleads guilty," Marie added. "In which case there will be no need for a trial."

He looked at her as if she had grown another head. "Sure. And Casey will stop knocking people down."

"Hey! I resemble that remark!"

He rolled his eyes and popped a French fry in his mouth.

"So it won't be goodbye for long," I said, happier than I'd been a minute before. I found that quite surprising.

"If the Whites won't let you rent the cottage," Mrs. Holmberg said, "you can stay with me."

"That is so sweet of you," I told her.

Larry returned in time to overhear my comment. "She is definitely sweet," he said with an affectionate wink in Mrs. Holmberg's direction.

"To seeing each other again," Norm toasted.

"Cheers!" we all called out, our glasses held up in friendship.

The End

Please help an author out and leave a review of this book at Amazon and/or Goodreads. Your help getting the word out is greatly appreciated.

Also by this author

Be sure to check out these other titles by Kelly Young.

Flurries Ending

Trumping the States

Living with Men

Kisses in the Moonlight: And Other Short Tales

From the Heart: A Lifetime of Poetry

Shades of Green: The Fraulein and the Handyman

The Mitten Tree

And look for the next book in The Travel Writer Cozy Mystery series, coming out in 2019!

About the author

Kelly Young was born in 1962 and has lived all over the great province of Ontario.

A graduate of the English literature program at the University of Waterloo, she moved to a small town on the shores of Lake Huron in southwestern Ontario with her husband, and together they raised two sons and a clowder of cats. She has since moved to a small city in further south southwestern Ontario, where she is trying out retired life.

Kelly worked as a freelance reporter for many years, switching to full time reporting for the local paper briefly before taking herself to a much quieter bookstore. After coaching two competitive swim teams, she worked at the municipal pool teaching people of all ages how to swim until her early retirement at age 55.

Kelly is an avid swimmer who tries to swim at least two times a week.

She currently rules over an empty nest with her husband and two cats.

Follow her on Amazon, Facebook, Twitter, Pinterest, LinkedIn, and Bookbub, request a digital autograph at Authorgraph, or visit her website at http://kyoung18.wixsite.com/kelly-young-author.

51142127R00130

Made in the USA
Middletown, DE
01 July 2019